CLOCKWISER

A YOUNG ADULT TIME TRAVEL ROMANCE

LEE STRAUSS

CLOCKWISER

a Clockwise Collection book

by Lee Strauss

(previously published under the names Elle Strauss and Elle Lee Strauss)

THE CLOCKWISE COLLECTION

Clockwise
Clockwiser
Like Clockwork
Counter Clockwise
Clockwork Crazy

1

CASEY

Beginning of Summer Holidays

SOMETIMES I JUST WISHED I were an only child. But then, I guess I'd be walking or taking transit instead of getting a lift from Tim in his Cavalier beater. He didn't have air conditioning either, and the wind blowing in from our open windows was hot and moist. The humidity made me feel like I was wearing a warm wet washcloth for a shirt.

"Can't you drop me off first?" I said, fanning myself with my hand. I was meeting my best friend Lucinda at the mall where she worked at Forever21 and she only had a forty minute break. Plus, there was the added bonus of air conditioning there. Tim stubbornly refused, insisting that he had to stop at the ATM for some cash first.

"I'm not your personal taxi service, Casey," he snarled, turning the volume up on his stereo. The bass beat was so loud it rattled the trunk. "Get off your lazy butt and get your license already."

I gave him a dirty look and reached over to turn the music down. I had a very good reason for not getting my license, one I could never tell Tim or any member of my family. There were only three people, *currently living*, that knew the reason why. One of them was my boyfriend, Nate MacKenzie.

My heart still fluttered a bit when I thought of him in those terms. *My boyfriend.* Not just some out of reach guy I crushed hard on my whole sophomore year who was totally out of my league, but my *boyfriend*.

We'd already been an official couple for an entire year, totally blowing all the doomsday predictions that we'd never make it. No one thought a college boy would stick it out with a junior in high school (especially Nate's former evil girlfriend!)

But he did, and we were still going strong. I'd be entering my senior year in a few weeks and then I'd go to Boston University, too.

"If you dropped me off first, you wouldn't have to deal with me." I tried to reason.

"If I didn't shuttle you around at all I wouldn't have to deal with you."

The only reason he did was because my parents were putting the screws in. Tim's bad attitude, questionable choice of friends and poor grades put him in their bad books. Driving me around was penance.

Tim pulled into the parking lot of the bank and hopped out, leaving the car running. I reached over and turned it off. Idling the car was bad for the environment for one, and a waste of Tim's hard earned minimum wage job money. You'd think he'd know better.

I checked the time on my phone and grew anxious as Lucinda's break time grew nearer. Tim had his back to me as he stood in line at the ATM window. I checked my reflection in the visor mirror. Since I'd grown out of my skinny awkwardness last year, (and of course, snagged a hot boyfriend) I was more mindful of my looks. Instead of trying to hide behind a bush of dark curly hair, I took care of it with hair products and good salon cuts. I was happy with the way my curls framed my face now. I took a tube of lip gloss out of my purse and rolled it onto my lips.

I tugged on my shorts and rubbed my bare legs. They were so long, my knees almost touched the glove compartment. Height had its advantages, but getting comfortable in a small car wasn't one of them.

I turned the radio on and hummed along with the top forty. I daydreamed about me and Nate and how we could relax for the rest of the summer, hopefully stretching the lazy days out as long as possible.

I checked the time on my phone and immediately started stressing about being late to meet Lucinda. C'mon, Tim! He was second in line now. I texted Lucinda to let her know I might be a little late.

I heard sirens in the area and I perked up. This wasn't the best neighborhood. The bank wasn't huge, just tucked into a strip mall along with a nail place, a dollar store, and a thrift shop. Litter overflowed from the bin and a good amount had been blown up against the cement foundation.

I checked on Tim. He'd finally made it to the front, the last one in line. If I'd known it was going to take him this long, I would've ran into the dollar store and picked up cheap nail polish.

The siren noise grew increasingly louder and suddenly three cop cars pulled into the parking lot beside me. My heart jumped and I thought fleetingly that maybe Tim was in trouble with the law again, except that he was getting money out of the ATM, not robbing the bank.

But someone was.

Everything happened so fast.

A guy with a ski mask pushed past Tim as he ran out the bank doors. A cop shouted, "stop or I'll shoot." Another masked man followed. Guns went off.

I heard myself shout, "Tim!" He was right in the middle of the cross fire!

He stood there, stunned and frozen. A police officer ran to him, pushing him to the ground, just as the second armed man shot in their direction. The officer fell to the ground taking the bullet instead of Tim.

The robbers ran around the corner and out of sight, chased by police officers on foot and a cruiser down the back alley.

I sprinted to Tim where he was on the ground by the fallen cop.

"Are you okay?"

His face was white and he motioned to the woman beside him. "Yeah, but I don't think she is."

The officer moaned, holding her hand on her chest.

"Oh, ma'am, are you okay?" I searched for blood but couldn't see any.

"I will be," she said gasping for breath. "I have a vest on."

Another officer kneeled beside her. "Ambulance is on its way."

The woman had dark hair pulled back in a low bun. Her eyes stayed pinched together and her pale face glistened with sweat. The impact of the bullet was enough to do some damage. I picked up her police hat that had fallen off her head and handed it to her.

"Thank you," I said.

"Just doing my duty."

The ambulance arrived. The paramedics pushed us aside and lifted the woman onto a gurney.

The cop who'd checked her pulse stepped forward from his opened door cruiser. Radio dispatch noises leaked out.

I watched the ambulance pull away, siren blasting, and realized I didn't know her name. I asked the officer standing beside me.

"That's Officer Clarice Porter," he said. "Now, would you two mind coming with me to the station to file a report?"

We agreed and I took my first ride in a police car. It was Tim's second, the first was not for noble reasons. He still claimed it was his friend Alex and not him that had stolen the cigarettes from the convenience store.

A thought like a loud banner ran through my mind as the doors of the police cruiser slammed shut and we drove away.

Clarice Porter saved my brother's life.

2

CASEY

One Month Later

NATE LIFTED MY CHIN (ah, I loved it when he did that) and I closed my eyes, waiting for the kiss.

I wrapped my arms around his neck and puckered up in anticipation, but before his tasty, soft lips touched mine, we were interrupted by a honking car and the most inconsiderate driver ever.

Tim screeched into the driveway with his signature blasting bass line vibrating his car, like he had someone trapped in the trunk and he was kicking it in rhythm from the inside. I imagined the whole neighborhood sighing with relief when he turned the engine off. His friend Alex hopped out the passenger door with a shrug and a limp wave before hoofing it the block and a half down the street to where he lived.

"Get a room," Tim grunted as he passed us.

"Oh, that's so original," I spouted back.

Nate frowned. "What's his problem?"

"Which one, he has many." I felt my shoulders droop. "You'd think that a near death experience would make you appreciate life more."

And the people in it. If anything Tim had gotten even surlier since the incident at the bank. My parents had contacted a counselor, but so far Tim had refused to go.

Nate's frown deepened. "He wasn't the only one who could've been hurt, you know. And here I thought I only had to worry about you when you tripped."

"Trip" was the word we used for when I traveled back in time to the nineteenth century. Yup, I time traveled. You can't get any more abnormal than that. But I was thankful for my "gift" now. It had everything to do with how Nate and I got together.

I didn't want Nate to worry about me, here or there. "Where were we?" I said, grabbing his waist and pulling him close.

He tilted his head towards mine. "I think we were just about to..."

I pursed my lips and let myself fall into the rhythm of his kisses.

Nate's mouth went to my ear. "I have to go or I'll be late for work."

Nate had a summer job working as a mail boy for an advertising corporation in Cambridge.

My fingers went to the cross around my neck as I watched him climb into his rusty '82 BMW and drive away. I blew out a long breath when he disappeared around the corner.

When I turned to go back to the house I stopped short.

Standing in the neighbor's driveway was Chase Miller. The Millers were new, just moved in next door two weeks ago. My parents had been quick to greet them and get all the facts. Turned out Chase was my age and would be going to Cambridge High with me in the fall. He was just barely my height, with short dirty blond hair. He had a slimmer build than Nate, and walked with a lazy, easy-going slouch. Still, there was something appealing about him. He had calming, dark-eyes and right now they were settled on me.

Had he been watching me and Nate kiss goodbye?

He leaned against a small car with his arms folded. He raised his eyebrows and flashed me an amused smile.

I felt myself blush and let my gaze fall to the driveway as I headed for the front door.

We lived in a large white Colonial with two rows of symmetrical windows, each with black slatted shutters. The flat yard had mature trees and bushes in full summer bloom, and was fenced in the back. Easily large enough for just the four of us, yet so often lately it didn't seem nearly big enough. Mom and Dad were recently reunited after a year-long separation. Tim used that difficult event to fuel his innate need to rebel which unfortunately hadn't subsided with Dad's move back home.

I could hear Mom shouting when I entered the front door. She and Tim were at it again. What was it this time?

Tim's voice carried down from the upper floor. "Why are you snooping in my room?"

My mother yelled back, "Are you going to try to blame this on your friends, too?"

I hated it when they fought. I thought it might help if I offered a diversion. "Hey Tim, can I get a ride to Lucinda's?"

He was already bounding down the steps and said tersely as he brushed by, "No."

Mom was on his heels. She stopped when she saw me, opening her hand to reveal the item in her palm. I grimaced. It appeared that Tim was into smoking more than just cigarettes these days. Mom closed her eyes, deflated. Why did Tim insist on hurting her? My blood surged with a new bout of anger and indignation and I chased after him.

"Tim! You're doing drugs now? Are you insane?"

"Leave me alone."

I couldn't believe Tim would do drugs. Even the mild stuff could tempt a stupid guy like Tim into trying something worse. I was furious. "Who's giving you drugs?"

I reached his car just as he started the engine. The window was down and I grabbed onto the door frame. Tim's hair had grown and constantly fell into his eyes. He flicked his head so he could see and that's when I noticed his black eye.

"What happened to you?"

He narrowed his good eye at me. "Nothing, let go of my car."

My heart raced. Why did Tim have to go off the deep end, just when things looked like they might get back to normal for this family?

"Drugs *and* fighting?" I spat out.

Tim revved the engine. "I said, let go of my car."

"Not until you answer me. Who's dealing?"

Tim grabbed my arm, pushing me out. I refused to let go. It was a bad idea.

A dizzy spell and a flash of light later, I was pulled to the ground by my brother. We were surrounded by mature, leafy deciduous trees. Small birds rustled away from a nest nearby. I breathed in deeply the scents of the warm earth and unpolluted air.

Tim shifted back and forth, taking in his new surroundings, his eyes bugging out like he was on a bad trip.

"Wh-what just happened? Where are we?"

I groaned because I knew where we were. We were in the middle of a forest in Cambridge Massachusetts in the year 1862.

3

CASEY

STRESS WAS MY BIGGEST TRIGGER. My sophomore year was majorly stressful, and I'd tripped back in time so often I'd lost count. My parents had split up and Tim had started this rebellious stage he was obviously still in and well, there was Nate. I also happened to be madly in love with him, and then he'd asked me to dance. I'd never dreamed in a million years I'd actually get to talk to him, much less touch him.

But now that Nate and I were a couple, things had sort of normalized. Nate went to college, I finished my junior year, and we fell into a routine that included a lot of time on the phone and dates on the weekends.

Dad moved back home, which I thought was great but Tim resented. I think he enjoyed how he could get away with things when only mom was around. But besides the odd misdemeanor and the permanent cloud around his head, things more or less ran smoothly.

Until this moment.

My mouth fell open as I stared at my brother who was on

his butt on the grass, leaning back on his hands, taut as a startled cat.

Oh, no. Oh, no, oh no.

Tim's good eyelid flickered madly. "Casey? What's going on? What happened to my car?"

I'd been traveling back to the nineteenth century off and on since I was nine. I'd brought my best friend Lucinda back once. That was how I found out I could bring people back if I happened to be touching their skin when I tripped.

I'd managed to go a whole eight years without bringing a family member back. This was new territory.

I jumped up and down a little, and gritted my teeth. What was I going to do *now*?

"Casey?" Tim's voice shook. "What the..."

"Okay," I said. "I'll explain. Um, I'm not sure how to say this, but we've traveled back in time."

I waited for Tim to say something. No words came out of his mouth but he was breathing heavily.

"I'm a time-traveler." I waved my hands a bit as if that would help him to understand. "It's this odd gift I have."

His face twisted in unbelief. "Are you on drugs, man?"

I huffed. "No."

He leaned forward and studied his hands, "Am I?"

"I wouldn't know the answer to that." I crossed my arms. "But we did trip. Just not that kind of trip."

I extended an arm. "Get up."

To my surprise, Tim took my hand without remark. I pulled him off the ground and he stood. We were the same height, nearing five-eleven. I used to hate that I was so tall, but I'm fine with it now.

I pulled my loose curly mane off of my face and tied it back with a hair band I had on my wrist.

"Let's go," I said.

Tim was sixteen months younger than me, and people often thought we were twins until I had my first growth spurt. I'd kept a steady six inches ahead of him for about five years. Then he spent a year being taller than me until I caught up again. Even though we were the same height, I still thought of him as my little brother. Now that we were in the past, the hard, tough guy edge he'd been carrying for the last couple years had melted away, at least temporarily. He looked like a lost little puppy. I almost felt like hugging him.

Almost.

"This is so messed," he said. He spun around to take in our surroundings. Pure unadulterated forest. Not a Colonial or Victorian style home in sight. "Where are we going?"

"Follow me. I have a stash near here."

Tim trailed me like a zombie. In fact, with that black eye, his bad posture, and his propensity to drool, he actually looked like a zombie. Maybe I should've been frightened.

I sneaked a peek over my shoulder. Nah. Just the regular, messed up Timothy Donovan that I'd known and loved my whole life.

I had to dodge and whack a path for us through new summer growth. I was always amazed how loud the wild was, with a zillion birds chirping and squawking, and I wondered what they'd think if they knew how humans would invade and demolish much of it over the next hundred and fifty years.

I spotted the lilacs in the distance and let out a comforting sigh. A little bit of respite waited for me there. It'd give me time to think about our next move.

The lilac grove concealed the entrance to a secluded patch of grass. A fallen log, half rotten and moss-covered, lay along a cold fire pit. The space was about twenty-five feet in circumference and completely closed in by heavy brush, new growth pressing inward making it feel smaller. Long ago I'd dug a hole in the ground near the back with a "borrowed" shovel to store my belongings. It was covered with a thatch of branches.

Tim slunk to the log, and stared blankly into space. I supposed he was in shock. I couldn't help but compare the difference between him and Nate the first time Nate came back with me. Where Tim seemed to believe my every word and was completely dazed out by the experience, Nate had been convinced I'd participated in some kind of prank with his friends. He hadn't believed my story until well into the second day.

Tim's legs were jumping with nerves. His good eye settled on me. "But, how? When?"

I knew what he wanted to know. How did it work, and when did it start happening. I gave him the short version, telling him the story of how it happened for the first time when I was nine, after Mom had tucked me in bed. I'd watched a scary-movie on the sly and night-time frights were enough to trigger a trip. I was only gone a couple of days, but I was scared out of my wits. Plus it had poured rain, soaking me through my pajamas to the bone.

"And when I came back," I said, like I was recounting a perfectly normal childhood memory, "I was in bed again at exactly the same time I'd left, wearing dry pajamas."

Time in the past went by at the same rate as the future. If there were two weeks between trips in the present, those same two weeks went by in the past. It worked differently the other way around. I could spend two weeks in the past, but I always returned to the same moment I left in the present.

Tim shook his head. "This is so crazy."

"Yeah, it is."

"Do Mom and Dad know?"

I gave him a sideways glance, "No, and don't you dare tell them."

"Does anyone else know?"

"Lucinda. I brought her once by accident, too. And Nate."

Tim's eyebrows shot up. "Nate Knows? And he still wants to go out with you?"

"Shut up."

I sat on the log beside Tim. I wasn't sure what to do now. I'd double checked the hole and there wasn't any food in there. I hadn't had a chance to re-stock it last time. The jar of water had been sitting unpreserved for several months.

"Where is the rest of civilization?" Tim said, looking around. "What year is it anyway?"

"It's 1862."

"Get out! The Civil War?"

I nodded.

"That is so cool."

"You're an idiot." I stood up, and stared hard at him. "The Civil War era was a terrible, barbaric time. Over 600,000 Americans died."

Tim shrugged. "People die in wars."

I worried about Tim, that all those war games he played on his computer had warped his sense of reality, numbed his conscience.

"This isn't a game."

He blew me off. "I never said it was."

I went to the hole and pulled out a burlap sack.

"So now what?" Tim said behind me. "Do we just wait it out? How long does it usually take for you to go back?

"I don't know." I tugged on the fabric in the bag and pulled it out. "Could be one day, could be ten."

"How do you know when it's going to happen?"

I shook out the dress I'd stored there in the spring. It smelled a little moldy. "Unlike the trip from the present to the past, where I'm totally caught off guard," I started, "I get a little warning when I'm about to go back to the present. I feel dizzy and the world goes opaque. I'll have a few minutes to warn you, so you can grab my arm. Just make sure you're touching my skin."

Tim finally noticed what I was doing. "What's that?"

"It's a dress suitable for this time period. I can't go out there dressed like I just arrived from the twenty-first century. I'd get arrested."

"You're really going to wear that thing?"

"Yes, I'm really going to wear it, now turn around."

Tim complied and I slipped out of my T-shirt and jeans, and pulled the dress on over my head. I did the buttons up on the back as far as I could reach; thankful for my long arms.

There was still plenty of daylight and the thought of hanging around here making subpar conversation with Tim as we grew increasingly hungrier and thirstier didn't appeal to me.

Besides, I missed the Watsons. I wondered how Sara was doing with that houseful of younger siblings, and if they'd heard from her brother Willie since he'd enlisted.

I gave Tim's clothing a cursory glance. He wore a plain black T-shirt long enough to cover the zipper of his jeans. He wouldn't exactly blend in, but he could pass as a poor farm hand. I found myself grinning at the thought of Tim actually chucking a bale of hay or attempting to milk a cow.

I motioned with my head. "Let's go."

Tim fell into step behind me without a word.

I could hear them marching before they came into view. I crouched into the ditch waving with my hand for Tim to do the same. Unlike Nate who blabbered aloud and bumbled about on his first trip (to be fair, he acted normally for someone in denial), Tim seemed to have an intrinsic sense of stealth.

We watched as a group of soldiers dressed in gray and blue Union Army attire marched by in alignment. I figured they were new recruits on their way to Boston.

We held our breath until they were almost out of range. We only needed a couple more minutes before it would be safe to follow the same road to the Watsons.

Then Tim did another stupid thing. He jumped up from our hiding spot and yelled, "Hey wait for me," and sprinted down the road after them.

4

TIM

CASEY PICKED UP HER WRINKLED, ankle-length skirt and ran after me.

"No! Tim, stop!"

A part of my brain somewhere deep and in the back knew I was acting irrationally. Again.

My parents were pushing me to see a shrink. They wanted to know the one answer I couldn't give them. Why? Why the rebellious, destructive, careless behavior?

But I didn't know.

Maybe I was just tired of life. School bored me, my parents bored me, and my friends bored me. Everyone thought my "near death" experience would've changed me, made me a nicer, sweeter person.

I wondered myself why it hadn't. Maybe there was a dark spot in my soul that wished I hadn't been saved.

But, hey, I was in the past now and that didn't happen every day. This was my chance to do something exciting and my dad was nowhere around to tell me what I could and couldn't do.

Unfortunately, there was still my sister.

"Are you crazy?" Casey shouted after me. "What are you doing?"

When she finally reached me, she was puffing like an old dog, like she never took Phys. Ed. or anything. Oh, right, she didn't do sports. She left that job to her uberjock boyfriend. Her face was as red as a tomato and her expression was so bloated and stern, I thought she might combust. I almost laughed.

By the time she got her breath back, it was too late to stop me. The group of soldiers had spotted us and parted, so the guy in charge could come for a chat.

"Is there a problem?" he said. He wore a blue jacket over gray pants, with a cap set crookedly on his head. He had one of those ugly handlebar mustaches, and he looked just like those wannabe actors who dressed in costume for the war enactments.

How did I know for sure they weren't actors and this wasn't just some kind of fantastic set up?

Except my sister wouldn't pull a prank like this. She was too upright and uptight for that kind of thing. Plus, she wouldn't go anywhere near my friends, so they couldn't be part of this either.

It couldn't be a bad drug trip because I hadn't taken any drugs. Unless someone put something in my drink?

Except, I hadn't been drinking.

Still, I studied my hands. They looked steady and real.

"Excuse me," the soldier, or a guy dressed as a soldier, said with a low, guttural voice. "Is everything all right?"

He turned towards Casey, and I spotted an old musket gun hanging off his back. It only looked about ten years old, not a hundred and fifty.

I couldn't stop staring at it. Its long, smooth wooden stock attached to the polished metal barrel was a thing of beauty. I'd give anything to be able to shoot it.

"We're fine, sir," Casey said, pushing her hair away from her face like that made her look older, or prettier or whatever.

The guy cleared his throat. "Son?" Seemed he didn't like me staring at his gun.

"I want to sign up," I said.

"What?"Casey squawked. "No he doesn't!"

I ignored her panicked look. "Yes, I do."

The soldier cleared his throat. "There's a recruitment officer in the military camp nearest your town."

She stepped in front of me. "I'm so sorry to have disturbed you. My brother can't join the army. He's not well. He... he has, uh, a learning disability."

"Pardon me?" The officer's bushy eyebrows lowered over his narrowing eyes.

Casey scowled at me. "He's not right in the head."

Oh, thanks, sis.

"In that case, we bid you good day, ma-am." He nodded at me and turned to leave.

I was about to stop him again, but Casey pulled on my arm, almost jerking it out of the socket. "Ow."

"Listen up," she snarled. "This is my gig. I call the shots."

She cracked me up with all her phoney intimidation. I made my eyebrows jump. "Ooh, scary."

"You should be scared. And you need to be with me to get home."

"Maybe I don't want to go home."

She shook her head, disgusted at me. As usual.

"You have no idea what it's like to live here." She counted

off her fingers. "There's no TV, no electricity, no running water, *no internet*. You got what I'm saying? This is *no* picnic."

Whatever. I had no choice but to follow her now. Despite the temptation to ditch her, I really didn't know my way around. Yet.

She sure had a bee up her butt. I almost had to jog to keep up with her and her swishing skirt.

"Okay, I'm sorry," I said. "That was dumb."

"No kidding."

The road we were stomping on was unpaved and unpopulated. The soldiers had disappeared ahead of us and the only thing I could tell for sure was that we were moving in an easterly direction.

"Where are we going?"

She slowed a little. "To the Watsons."

"Like, actual people?"

"Yeah, like actual people."

Casey wiped sweat off her brow with the long sleeve of her dress. She looked worn out and tired, but I felt like I was on fire, a helium balloon tied to the ground but reaching for the sky.

"What are we going to do when we get there?" I said, trying to restrain the spring in my step.

"Work,"

"Work?"

"Yes, work," she said with an exasperated breath. "You know that thing you do for room and board. Oh, yeah, you don't. Well, you're in for a rude awakening. No free ride here."

"Hey, I know how to work." I worked delivering pizza on Saturday nights.

She huffed and shot me a look of doubt.

It felt like we walked forever, but at least the temperatures had dipped and I no longer had to keep pulling my clinging shirt from my damp chest. Eventually, we came to a farm. A big house sat in from the road with an American flag attached to one of the gables that flapped gently in the wind. Behind it was a barn and a small lake. A bunch of kids ran around the yard, and I spotted workers out in the fields.

"This it?" I said. Casey nodded stiffly. Seemed I still wasn't forgiven.

Casey walked up the drive like she'd been there a dozen times. Maybe she had. She said she'd been doing this on and off for eight years. I still couldn't wrap my head around this whole time travel story.

That was the stuff of science fiction.

Or maybe just science. I'd heard that it could be possible to shift time if you moved faster than the speed of light or fell into a wormhole or something.

I didn't understand what happened with Casey or how it worked, but I couldn't deny that my day to day surroundings had suddenly changed and in a big way.

A redheaded girl, a little older than Casey, was outside hanging clothes on a line. She wore a long dress similar to what Casey had on, and an apron. Another re-enactment actor? That was just as hard to believe as the notion we'd gone back in time.

When she spotted us, she dropped a shirt into a basket and walked our way.

"Cassandra?"

I glanced at Casey, questioning.

"That's what they call me here," she said under her breath. Casey embraced the redhead, who looked a little embarrassed by her outburst of emotion.

"It's been a long time," the redhead said.

"Yes, it has, but it's so good to see you again, Sara," Casey gushed. She finally remembered I was with her. "Oh, this is my brother, Tim, uh, Timothy."

"You brought another brother?" Then to me. "Nice to meet you, Timothy."

I wasn't sure what behavior was expected of me. I just nodded my head and mumbled, "Thanks."

Sara turned back to Casey. "Nathaniel isn't with you this time?"

Nathaniel? That's what they called Nate? I chuckled in my head. Then I registered the rest of her previous sentence. "He's not her br..."

"Sara," Casey cut me off. "It's Timothy's first time out of Springfield. He's a little socially..." she lowered her voice, "awkward. Don't mind him."

"Very well," Sara said throwing me a concerned look. "Come in for refreshments."

It looked like the wide-opened back door led to the kitchen, if I could go by the long, wooden table I spotted inside. Just as we were about to enter, we ran into a girl about my age. She also wore a long dress, but she filled it out in a way that made her look hot. She resembled Sara but had long dark hair that hung in waves around her face. She gasped slightly when she saw me, but then her eyes smiled.

"Josephine, you remember Cassandra?" Sara said. She motioned to me. "And this is another one of her brothers, Timothy."

"Hello," she said shyly. My heart skipped a beat. I flashed her a lopsided grin, aware that my purple eye just added to my bad boy appeal. She smiled in return, her eyes sparkling in the way that confirmed a mutual interest.

Things had suddenly taken an interesting turn here in the past. I thought I just might like hanging out at the Watsons' after all.

5

CASEY

"JOSEPHINE?" I said, trying not to stare at her ample breasts that had sprouted sometime in the last year. "Wow, you're all grown up."

"Hello, Cassandra."

I wasn't the only one staring. I saw the glint in Tim's eye, and I gave him a sharp elbow nudge as we followed Sara into the kitchen. Wherever Josephine had intended to go, she'd changed her mind and followed us back in. I still couldn't believe her transformation. She was at least fifteen by now. Younger than Tim, but judging by the eager look on his face, he wasn't too concerned about that.

Dumb hormones. Now I have *that* to worry about, too. Tim was already proving to be way more trouble than Nate ever was.

The kitchen still had the lingering sweet scent of break-fast. I sat in my usual spot on the back side along the long wooden table, with Tim weirdly in Nate's old place. Sara opened the chrome door of the wood fire stove and stoked the orange embers that remained. She touched a kettle on the top and deemed it to be hot, then poured the water into a teapot.

Josephine busied herself by providing a plate of biscuits; but she didn't hide the fact that she was stealing glances at Tim as well. Tim was also being too bold, and I kicked him under the table. He grunted.

Other younger Watson kids of various sizes with either dark or red hair ran through the kitchen with Mrs. Watson on their heels. "Get outside," she said. "It's too nice to be indoors."

She stopped when she saw me. "Why hello, Cassandra." Mrs. Watson was a petite woman with a salt and pepper bun at the back of her head. She'd had her tenth child, Daniel, over a year ago and I'd had the surprising experience of helping Sara deliver him.

"Hi, Mrs. Watson," I said with a smile, "How are you?"

"Good, all things considered, what with this terrible war going on."

Which reminded me of Willie, the oldest Watson son. I waited for Sara to join us with the tea and once we'd all been served and the sugar passed around, I asked about him.

"Willie's here, actually," Sara said. "He'd been injured at Shiloh, but he's now nearly fully recovered." She sighed. "So many men died in that battle. Willie was part of the re-enforcement regiment that came the second day and forced the Confederates back."

I felt myself let go of a long breath. I hated that he'd been injured but I was relieved to hear he was okay. "I can't wait to see him again."

"I'm sure he feels the same way," Mrs. Watson said. She smiled sadly. "Now that he's well again, they've sent notice that he must return to his regiment."

Sara turned to her sister. "Josephine, go fetch Willie from the barn."

Josephine's smile turned into a pout. "Why should I have to? Ask one of the children to do it."

Mrs. Watson gave her daughter a stern look. "Go on. It'll only take you a minute."

Josephine barely concealed her huff, waves of dark hair bouncing on the back of her cotton dress. I took in Tim's smirk and shook my head.

"It's been a beehive of activity around here, since the war started," Sara said. "Boston is full of soldiers coming and going from their tours, and business in town is booming. Is it like this in Springfield?"

I nodded lightly. "Um, yes, but..."

"Has Nathaniel enlisted? Is that why you brought Timothy this time?"

"Um, yes." I supposed this was as good of a story as any. Thankfully, Tim kept his mouth shut, but I could tell by the way his eyebrows arched that he'd be asking questions later.

Willie and Mr. Watson came through the door like a blast of wind. Willie was a younger, thinner version of his dad, but both had bushes of red curls on their heads and wide smiles on their faces. Behind them was a dark haired boy I recognized as another Watson kid, Duncan.

"Cassandra! So good to see you." I stood in greeting, and Willie took my hand, lifting it quickly to his lips.

"So good to see you, too," I said. "And that you are still alive and well."

Willie, Duncan and Mr. Watson moved their chairs noisily, and sat.

"Us, too," Mr. Watson said, his voice booming in the large

room "We are grateful to God that our boy is back safe and sound."

"For now," Willie said, stirring his tea. "I must leave again shortly."

"When, exactly are you leaving?" Tim said, out of the blue.

"Four days," Willie answered. "And you are?"

"Oh, sorry," I jumped in. "This is my brother, Timothy."

"Another brother," Willie said. "Great to meet you. Good timing as Father will need an extra hand when I leave."

"Yes, indeed," Mr. Watson said. Tim only nodded. Boy, was he in for a surprise come morning when the rooster crowed.

If we were still here.

I really hoped we weren't still here. I needed to get Tim back home where Mom and Dad could stress over him, not me. And I already missed Nate, though he'd never even notice I was gone.

The playful staring going on between Tim and Josephine was starting to make me ill, but then the table conversation settled on the war.

"The Confederate Army is proving to be more resilient that we'd originally thought," Mr. Watson said.

Willie took a sip of his black coffee and agreed. "The Union made a significant error in judgement, completely underestimating their determination. The Confederates are like a dog with a bone. They are not going down without a fight."

"But will they be defeated?" Mrs. Watson questioned, her brow wrinkled with worry. "How long will this dreadful war go on?"

I was the only one at that table who knew the answer to

that question. Well, and Tim, but judging from his low American History marks, I wouldn't bet on it.

Mr. Watson pushed away from the table. "Time to get back to work. The cows don't wait for milkin'."

Willie's eyes settled on Tim. "Join us when you're ready."

Sara left the room and returned shortly with a stack of linen in her hands. "The cabin's empty. Here are some clean sheets."

I took them from her. "Thanks. I know the way."

THE COTS WERE STRIPPED and all the surfaces wiped down. The fireplace ashes were gone, but the blanket I had strung like a curtain down the middle of the tiny room for privacy remained.

"Home away from home," I said. I tossed Tim his sheets and went about making my bed. Then I flopped on my back, suddenly exhausted.

"This is pretty wild, Casey." Tim did a half baked job of making his bed and I fully expected all of it to fall haphazardly onto the floor before he woke up in the morning.

"I know, believe me I know, "I muttered.

Tim sat on the edge of his bed when he finished, hands on knees that jiggled up and down. I wanted to reach over and put a hand on him to stop his movements, but instead I just closed my eyes.

"So, you have this whole other life," he said, "this other family."

"Yeah, I'm very fortunate that the Watsons have taken me in like one of their own. We've had a few bonding moments."

"So what's up with the formal names?"

"Sara didn't think Casey was feminine enough, so she

christened me Cassandra. When Nate ended up here with
me I just thought it fitting that he should have a long handle
to deal with, too."

"Why do they think he's your brother?"

"Because, you can't hang out with the opposite sex
without a chaperone unless you're siblings. Oh, that reminds
me." I turned onto my side and propped up my head with
my hand. "You need to know our story."

"Our story?"

"We live in Springfield, and our mother just had our thirteenth sibling."

"Thirteenth! Man, Casey, why so many?"

"I needed to come across desperate. Why else would a
girl leave her own family to look for work? Besides they're
not real. Oh, I totally forgot, but I'd told Sara the baby's
name was Timothy. I hope she doesn't remember that."

"What baby?"

"Number thirteen. It doesn't matter. We're poor is all that
matters. And Nate, Nathaniel, is our older brother."

"Wait a minute," Tim's eyes narrowed as he considered
something. "Nate stayed here, in this cabin, with you?"

"Yeah, so what of it?"

"Just, you guys don't exactly act like siblings, if you know
what I mean."

"Well, we did then. Besides, he had a girlfriend at the
time." I scowled a little at the thought of the empty-headed
beauty queen, Jessica Fuller. She'd moved on to some college
guy who thankfully was going to a different college than
Nate.

Tim kicked his shoes off and tested out his cot, folding
his arms behind his head. "So, my sister's a time-traveler. I'd

never thought I'd say this, but you've jumped a hundred plus points on the cool-o-meter."

"Happy to impress you finally."

"What does this mean, though? You're messing around in the past. How do you know you're not going to change history or something?"

I repeated the theory I'd shared with Nate when he'd asked this same question. "I figure since in the present, I've already been back here, nothing I do here will change that. Everything I'll do, I've already done. You know, when I'm there."

"So, you're not worried about inadvertently starting the third world war, because if you had, we'd already have had a third world war in our present?"

"Something like that."

"Does that mean you don't have to be afraid of dying here, either?"

"I suppose not, but that doesn't mean I'd go off and do something stupid to prove it."

Time travel was such a brain game and physically exhausting as well. I just wanted to sleep, but Sara was expecting me in the kitchen. And Tim was expected in the barn.

"We should go." I pulled myself up into a seated position. Then I remembered the most important thing I needed to tell Tim.

"If I call you, come as fast as you can, okay? It means I'm feeling the trip home coming on. Just grab my hand."

Tim saluted, "Gotcha."

"Come on. I'll show you the barn."

The barn door stood ajar, and I breathed in deeply when

we stepped inside. There was something comforting about the smell of hay and animal sweat.

There were a few horses in the front stalls, and the milking cows were in the back. Overhead was a loft filled with hay where some of the workers slept overnight. I'd been known to sleep there myself on occasion when I could still pull off looking like a boy.

Willie sat on a three-legged stool beside one of the cows, all of which I called Betsy. "Hey," he said.

"I'm just showing Timothy around before I head to the kitchen," I explained.

"Sure." Willie stood and lifted two full tin pails of milk by their handles. "Do you mind finishing up?" He looked at Tim, and motioned to the cow nearest the door. "She's the last one that needs milking."

Willie left and Tim's eyes bugged open. He had no clue how to milk a cow.

"Here, I'll show you how." I grabbed an empty bucket and pulled the stool up to the last cow. "Now pay attention. Sara's waiting for me in the kitchen."

I showed him how to hold onto the teats (gently but firmly) and pull in a rhythm. "Think of your favorite song in a four-four beat."

The cow's tail flicked behind her, but I dodged out of its way. "It's okay, Betsy," I said, soothingly. The *thwack, thwack, thwack* sound of the milk hitting the bottom of the tin pail, the familiar sound, calmed her.

"Wow, Casey. Your skill set is impressive. I can see now how you managed to snag a guy."

I shot him a blistering glare, then stood and crossed my arms. "Your turn."

Tim took my place and reached tentatively for the cow's under belly.

"This is gross," he complained.

"Just do it."

Betsy's discomfort at his lack of confidence and skill was evident in how her tail flicked, smacking Tim in the head.

"Ouch!"

I laughed out loud. He deserved that. "I'll leave you to figure it out. Bring the pails to the kitchen when you're done.

I couldn't stop chuckling. That could take a while. Poor Betsy.

WE SURVIVED THE FIRST DAY, falling asleep within seconds of hitting the mattress. Hard work and fresh air did that to you. The next morning came much sooner than either Tim or I would've liked.

"I'm going to shoot that stupid rooster," Tim said, as I nudged him to get up.

I sent him out to the barn before heading towards the kitchen. I hoped he'd do better with the milking today. Yesterday's effort was dismal, and I covered for him the best I could.

Sara and I had porridge on the table before the guys came in from the barn. Josephine was helping Mrs. Watson sort out the needs of the younger kids.

I flashed Tim a questioning look when he followed Duncan and Willie into the kitchen. *How'd it go?* He just shook his head and scowled.

By mid-morning the kitchen was stifling hot, and I had to wipe my brow with my sleeve every two seconds. I peeled vegetables for the evening meal, slicing and cubing them before adding them to a pot of water where they'd sit until it was time to cook. Sara worked with me, ordering various kids around to help prepare lunch. We didn't have a lot of time to talk, but I did ask her about Robert Willingsworth, a man whom Sara had liked but who'd wanted to marry me instead. He turned out to be bad news for both of us.

"Oh, I heard he's gone south to side with the Confederates, but…" her lips turned up shyly. "I've met someone else."

"Really?"I smiled with excitement. "I knew there was someone better out there for you. What's his name?"

"Henry Abernathy. His father owns a bank in Boston. Our fathers do business together. That's how we met. He's very handsome and a real gentleman."

"Ah, Sara, I'm so happy for you." And I really was. It'd killed me to see how heartbroken she was over the Robert Willingsworth fiasco.

"I am happy," she said, though her smile dimmed.

"What's wrong?"

Her eyes glistened with tears. "He's enlisted."

"Oh, Sara."

"He says the draft is coming to the north just like it did in the south, so he might as well get his three years of service over with. Do you really think it's going to last three years, Cassandra?"

I knew the answer was yes, but I just shrugged, wishing there was something I could say to comfort her.

"I asked him not to enlist, to wait, just in case. But he says he wants to do his duty for the Union. Of course, that's very noble of him and one of the reasons I…"

"You love him," I finished for her.

She blushed. "Yes. I do."

I forced a smile to my face. "I'm sure everything will work out fine."

LUNCH WENT OFF WITHOUT A HITCH. Tim looked even more shocked from all the sudden hard labor that came with running a farm, but he was holding up exceptionally well, everything considered. He didn't even flinch when Duncan told him they were heading out to work the fields for the rest of the day.

For me, working for the Watsons consisted mainly of food prep, kitchen clean up, and more food prep... an endless cycle. The winters were miserable because of the cold, and the summers because of the heat. I felt flushed, and worried that I was leaving a trail of sweat in my wake.

I offered to get water from the pump out back, in the hopes of encountering a cool breeze passing amongst the bordering trees. I pumped the heavy steel handle until water started pouring out, then I cupped my hands to collect it. I slurped it back, relishing the coolness that ran down my throat. I filled the pail, wishing I could just lie back in the shade, but the guys would be back for supper soon.

I took a few moments to splash water on my face. It felt cool and refreshing but instead of rejuvenating me, I felt faint and a little dizzy.

I snapped to attention. "Tim!

I ran to the cabin hoping he'd returned early. I saw his work boots by the door, but he wasn't there. I quickly scanned the loo and finding it empty, I ran toward the barn. "Tim! Come now!

The barn door was opened and I peeked in. Besides the

animals, it appeared empty. Then I heard giggling coming from the loft.

"Tim!" I climbed up the ladder as fast as I could in a skirt. The first thing I saw when my eyes peered over the edge was Tim lying in the hay with his arm around Josephine, a finger to his lips as if to "shush" me.

"Tim!"

"Wow, take it easy," Tim said casually, mistaking me for being angry that I had caught him making out with a Watson. Josephine blushed and buried her face in the hay.

Good thing. She missed seeing me disappear into thin air.

Tim hadn't, though. He saw the whole thing, and he heard me screaming, too.

6

CASEY

I STOOD THERE SCREAMING. My hands gripped the driver's door of my brother's car, the engine was running and there was *no driver!*

My feet did a little tap dance. I pinched myself. I came back without Tim. I left my brother in the nineteenth century! I willed myself, *go back, go back, go back!*

Come on! If this wasn't stress, then I didn't know what was. Why couldn't my body just listen to me for once?

"Casey?"

I jumped at my mother's voice.

"Have you seen, Tim?" she continued, not noticing the absolute panic I tried to erase from my face. "I'm not finished with him."

I hid my raccoon eyes, the dark circles I got every time I returned from a trip, behind my curls. "Uh, nope, I haven't...I don't know..."

Mom moved from the doorway to the front step. She was the shortest member of our family by a good number of inches, and she kept her blond hair short and spiky. She wore a loose floral blouse over a denim skirt and flip-flops on her feet, looking every bit the home design artist she was.

"Why is Tim's car running? Where is he?"

"Um," I mentally raced for an excuse. "I was just fooling around...trying it out... in case I..."

"Just tell him to come find me. It's better for him if we can talk this out before your father gets home."

I nodded quickly and breathed out long and hard when she turned and went back into the house. I slid into the driver's seat and turned off the engine. My fingers gripped the steering wheel and my mind raced. What to do, what to do?

Glancing in the rear-view mirror, I saw my darkened eyes and my hair springing every which way. What a wreck.

Normally, when I got back from a trip, I'd head straight to bed, overcome with exhaustion, but this time my nerves were peaking. I could run a marathon on the adrenaline pumping through my body.

My bag still lay on the driveway where I'd dropped it in anger. I leaned out of the car to reach it and pulled it onto my lap. I dug out my cell phone and called Nate.

"Miss me already?" His voice was soothing and sexy. I took a breath, trying to calm myself.

"I went back."

"Back where?"

"*Back.*"

"Oh." Nate paused and I knew what he was thinking.

It was the first time since we'd officially been together that I'd gone back without him. And every single time he'd gone back with me, I'd gotten into trouble.

"So, you're back now," he finally added. "I can assume everything went all right?"

"No, everything's not all right. I took Tim back!"

"Tim? How... oh, forget it. You can tell me later. Is he freaked out? I bet that messed up his self-centered world a little."

"No, he's still self-centered. He's just not here."

There was another pause while Nate took that in. "You mean..."

I let out a sob, so unsexy sounding. "Yes, I left him there."

"I'm coming right over. Don't move."

I didn't know what Nate thought he could do. I wouldn't mind a hug and a few re-assuring if not accurate words. But I loved that he wanted to be here for me.

"Aren't you at work?" I asked.

"I'll tell them I'm sick, just don't worry."

Tim would be all right. I mean, what could possibly happen to him. He'd have to make up an excuse for my absence–at least he saw me go, he knew what happened to me–and he'd just have to wait it out until I got back, working with Mr. Watson and Duncan on the farm.

I closed my eyes and breathed deeply. Yes, it would be all right.

I heard the engine of a car drive up, and I turned my head, excited to see Nate. But it wasn't him. It was my dad.

"Hi, Casey," he said, eyeing me as I sat in Tim's car.

Tim and I got our height from our father and I got his dark curly hair, though he kept his shaved so short you'd never guess what kind of hair he had. "What are you doing?"

"Uh, nothing. Just dreaming."

He paused to take the image in, me in the driver's seat of a car. "Why don't you get your own license, Casey? I wouldn't be worried about you."

Oh, but you should, Dad, you should.

"Yeah, I'm just not ready yet," I said.

"Your mother called me." He shifted his briefcase to his other hand. "She's upset about Tim again. Do you know what he did now?"

I didn't want to get into Tim's issues with Dad. I just shook my head. Dad huffed and headed for the front door.

Finally Nate arrived, parking his BMW right behind me. I heard him cut his engine, then slam his door as he jumped out and moved to the passenger's side of Tim's car. He slid in and gave me a much appreciated hug. I let myself relax into him, catching my breath for the first time since I came back without my stupid brother.

If Mom or Dad happened to peek out the living room window and saw us, they'd be wondering at the sight of us hanging out together in Tim's car, but I couldn't seem to move.

"He's going to be all right, right?" I whimpered into Nate's shoulder.

Nate rubbed my back, "Sure."

But I knew what he was thinking. Since when did Tim ever NOT get into trouble? If he didn't go looking for it, it came looking for him.

I started to tremble. "Oh, Nate, if anything happens to him, it'll be my fault. I don't think I could forgive myself."

"Nothing's going to happen to him. He can be an idiot sometimes, but he's not stupid."

Right. Tim may not be the wisest creature on earth but he was intelligent. He'd figure things out.

"Tell me what happened."

I related the episode that led up to my taking Tim back in the first place.

"Ah, man." Nate gave my hand a squeeze. "And why couldn't Tim get to you in time?"

"He was making out with Josephine in the barn."

Nate's face scrunched up in disbelief. "What?"

"That's the idiot coming out in him."

"But, she's just a girl."

I huffed. "Not anymore. You could say she's blossomed since we last saw her."

Nate scratched his chin. "How long were you there?"

"Two days."

"Man, the kid didn't waste any time."

I shook my head. "You know what, he *is* stupid!"

I pulled away, letting myself slump against the car seat. Nate drummed his fingers on the dash.

"There must be a way to trigger you, to set off a trip," he said. He gave me a long look. "And you'd better be touching me when it happens."

I almost cried then. I was so happy to have Nate, that he knew about this side of my life, and that he was good with it. That he wanted to help, even if it meant going back to the nineteenth century with me.

"I was so stressed when I returned without him; I thought for sure I'd just shoot right back. But come to think of it, I've never had a back-to-back trip. Still, time keeps marching on there, you know? We have to figure out a way to get back, and soon."

Speaking about time passing quickly, suddenly Mom was calling me in for supper. When she saw Nate, she invited him to come in, too.

He hedged but I begged him.

"Please?" I grabbed his thigh. "I need your moral support when my parents go off about Tim. How am I going to explain why he doesn't show? They know he wouldn't leave without his car."

Nate's eyes fell to my hand gripping his leg.

"Okay, I'll come."

I let him go, vowing to stop acting like a crazy person.

"Thanks," I breathed out slowly.

I let out a long sigh as we headed for the front door, already knowing how this day would play out. The police would be called by the end of the night.

7

TIM

"WHOA, JUST WHOA...." I sprung to my feet sending a cloud of hay dust through the air.

Josie straightened her skirt, and fussed with her hair. "Where'd your sister go?"

I rushed to the rail, scanning the barn floor and wondering if Casey fell off the ladder. But somehow my gut told me it was much worse than that. I went to the loft window and searched the yard, hoping in vain she'd be running across it for some reason.

Nope. Just a few playful Watson kids.

I hadn't imagined it. It really happened. Casey just vanished before my eyes. I laced my fingers behind my head and let out a long sigh.

"Man, bad luck."

Josie scurried up beside me. "Oh, my goodness! She's not going to tell Sara or my mother, is she?"

"No," I said slowly. "We won't have to worry about that."

It hit me that maybe I'd been just a little too reckless. Josie was cute and everything but not worth getting left behind a hundred and fifty years in the past for. I'd messed up pretty bad. I suddenly felt light-headed. I needed to lie down, process what had just happened.

"Hey, Josie," I said. She frowned. I didn't think she liked it when I called her that, but she didn't tell me to stop.

"I think I'm going to go clean up for supper."

"Yes, you are right. I must make leave of you as well." She blushed when she said it, and I couldn't stop myself from brushing a loose strand of hair from her face. This set off an adorable giggle.

I let her go down the ladder first.

"I'll see you soon," I said, then I jumped the last few rungs to the floor.

Her eyes widened with concern. "You'll talk to your sister?"

"Yeah, she'll be cool."

Josie's face went blank. "She's cold? Should I provide another blanket?"

"No, I mean, she'll understand."

Back in the cabin I fell onto the hard cot, groaning along with the creak of the worn out springs. I slipped my hands behind my head, stared at the wood-beam ceiling, and focused on a few deep, long breaths. Everything would be okay. Casey would come back for me. I just needed to bide my time, wait it out. And, at least I had Josie to keep me company.

If I hadn't been so famished, I would've skipped supper altogether just to avoid the questioning that was sure to come about my missing sister, but my stomach overruled.

Everyone was gathering around the table by the time I entered. Sara shot me a look.

"Cassandra didn't return from fetching water. Have you seen her?"

I took a seat and lowered my eyes. "Yeah, she's not well. Some flu or something. Came on really fast."

"Should I send someone to tend to her?" Before I could answer she called for Josie.

"No," I said, "Case, uh, Cassandra was very clear about wanting to be left alone."

Sara paused, then nodded. "Very well, then."

The kitchen filled with the sounds of chair legs scraping along the wooden floor, the bickering between little kids, and the final additions of dishes to the table. Then Mr. Watson called his family to order to pray over the food.

AFTERWARDS, I headed back to the cabin smacking at the army of mosquitoes that appeared with dusk. Inside I struck a wooden match against a matchbox, sniffing in the faint smell of phosphorus, and held it to the wick of the candle. I sat up on the cot with my back against the wall and watched the shadows cast by the small flame flicker about the room.

It was strangely quiet, until my ears tuned into the sounds of the outdoors. Crickets. A hoot of an owl. Another noise I couldn't identify. My nerves sprung awake. What kind of wild animals populated the forest around here, anyway? Could there be thieves wandering about?

It was probably just the wind, but I went to the door to lock it. It didn't have a locking mechanism. Had locks not been invented yet?

I took the wooden chair in the corner and propped it up under the handle. Back on my bed, I twiddled my thumbs.

Actually *twiddled*. I itched to have my laptop to play *War of the Universe*. The nineteenth century was *boring*, man.

Truth be told, it was kind of freaky being alone in a dark cabin on the edge of the woods at night. No streetlights or neon signs. No music. Too bad I didn't have my iPod with me. Wouldn't Josie freak out if she saw that?

I smiled at the thought of her cute little upturned nose and bright eyes. Not to mention her curvy body. Even that nightgown she wore all day couldn't hide it.

I shucked in under my blankets and then remembered I should blow out the candle. Last thing I needed was to burn down the cabin and me with it.

Too bad Casey wasn't here. As super annoying as she was, I wouldn't have minded her company right now. I didn't like how the blanket that hung in the middle of the room moved like there was someone behind it.

I lit the candle again, and tore it down, throwing it onto Casey's bed.

That was better.

I tossed and turned, miffed that the cot was so hard. How was a guy supposed to sleep?

Finally I dozed off, and it felt like I'd slept all of ten minutes. Next thing I knew, the sun shone brightly through the window and I heard the rooster crow. I covered my head with my pillow and rolled over.

Then a knock on the door with Duncan's voice coming from behind. "Timothy, are you in there? Pa is getting antsy."

I forced my eyes to open and pushed myself into a standing position. Last thing I needed was to get booted off the farm. What would I do if I couldn't stay here?

I dressed quickly and ran across the yard, trying to make up for lost time. Sara confronted me at the kitchen doorway, her red hair pulled back tightly with two ropes of braids running down her back. Someone should tell her that wasn't an attractive look.

"Where's Cassandra?" she asked. "Is she still ill?"

Man. I should've spent some time working on an excuse. Being sick wasn't going to account for her being missing.

"She's better now, but she had to go."

"She had to go?"

"Um..."

"Was there another family crisis?"

I stared at my boots. "Uh, yeah, I guess so."

"And she went by *herself*?" Sara shook her head sharply. She had her tea towel twisted so tightly I thought she might whip my legs. I took a step back.

"I would've sent someone with her," she huffed. "Why doesn't she ever say goodbye?"

I offered an apologetic shrug.

"Go on in," she motioned to me. "There's some oatmeal left on the table, but don't dawdle. You're expected in the barn."

I held back from saying "Yes, ma'am." And I certainly didn't *dawdle*.

Man, I was starving again. Must be all this fresh air. I scooped a glob of cold porridge into a bowl and frowned. Not too appetizing. I piled on the brown sugar and super thick milk and forced it down.

Josie was there, feeding a little brother. She sneaked glances at me and I smiled discreetly. Though maybe not discreetly enough. Sara cleared her throat and knitted her red eyebrows.

I shoved the last spoonful into my mouth and carried my

dirty dishes to the sink, an action that seemed to surprise her, if her eyebrow activity was anything to go by.

I ran across the back yard, puffing lightly as I entered the barn.

Mr. Watson saw me and said, "Tomorrow you will arrive for breakfast on time. That's not a suggestion."

"Yes, sir" I wondered if it would be impertinent to ask for an alarm clock.

Mr. Watson handed me a pitchfork and I followed him and Duncan out to a horse and cart. Mr. Watson straddled the horse whose mane was nearly the same color as Mr. Watson's red hair. He nudged the horse's flanks and trotted off. Apparently me and Duncan were walking.

Duncan pointed. "We're weeding the potato field."

I nodded, already anticipating the blisters I'd have on my hands by the end of the day. I followed him until we reached the field, and watched him dig into the earth between rows. Then I mimicked him.

I wondered why Willie hadn't joined us, so I asked Duncan. "Did he leave already?"

"Nah, he's fixing up the chicken coop. Lucky son of a gun." Duncan covered his eyes with one hand from the glare of the morning sun.

"Cleaning the chicken coop makes him lucky?"

"No, he's lucky because he's over eighteen."

I still wasn't getting it. "So?"

"When you're eighteen you can join the army." He said this like it was something I should already know, which explained the odd look that came before it.

I grabbed a fistful of weeds and threw them into a pile. "I thought he almost got killed? Isn't that a reason to avoid the army?"

"Nah, his injuries weren't serious." He tossed me a sly grin. "Just enough to get the girls all crazy over him."

Duncan took a hanky out of his pocket and wiped the sweat from his brow. I did the same.

"Plus," he continued, "it gets him off this farm doesn't it? He gets to have an adventure, shoot guns, fight for the glory of the Union."

I loosened the earth with my pitchfork, bent down and plucked out more weeds. "That does sound exciting."

"And can you think of a better way to impress girls than to show up at a party dressed in your army uniform? The girls almost faint over a man in a uniform."

"You got a point there, Duncan. Where do we sign up?"

"I can't. I'm only sixteen." His gaze settled on me. "How old are you?"

"Eighteen," I said without hesitation, though I was actually the same age as Duncan. That's the thing about being tall, people always think you're older than you are. Plus, my facial hair was filling out. I rubbed my chin, satisfied with the bristles I felt there.

The field grass we were weeding made me sneeze like every two minutes and drove me crazy. Stupid allergies. My eyes itched and it was all I could do not to stop pitching weeds, and pull my eyeballs out of my head.

Duncan laughed at me.

"Hang in there, Timothy," he said. "Soon we will hear the midday meal bell."

I wondered if Casey would be back at the house by then. Just how long would it be before she came back for me?

Then I realized I didn't know how this time travel thing worked. It wasn't like there was a button she could push.

How much time went by in between her "trips?" Man, I couldn't believe I hadn't asked her these things.

I didn't mind playing farm boy for a day, but I was ready to go home. I craved a grilled sandwich on white bread with processed sliced cheese and tomato soup that only required a can-opener to make.

Casey wasn't there when the noon bell rang for lunch.

And she didn't show up for supper, a thick vegetable stew and bread as heavy as a brick.

Josie made eyes at me across the kitchen but I was in no mood for fooling around. My eyeballs still burned, and I needed a shower, bad. I was exhausted and right about the prediction of blisters on my hands.

When I got back to the cabin, I slammed the door and smacked it with my fist. Was I going to be left here for good? Well, at least my parents wouldn't have to deal with their problem child anymore. Casey could have the happy family unit she'd been crying for these past two years without me around to stir up trouble.

I used the outhouse behind the cabin, which was no fun in the dark of night–I'd forgotten to bring the candle with me. Then I washed up with water I had to pump out of the ground myself.

The hard cot suddenly felt like a feather bed. I closed my eyes and a second later the sun was up and the rooster crowed.

I groaned. At home I pushed the snooze button on my alarm a dozen times and then waited for Mom to rag on me.

But I didn't want to face the wrath of Mr. Watson, and I had no choice but to stick it out here. Where would I go if they kicked me out, and how would Casey find me when she came back?

If she came back.

The third day wasn't any better than the first two. In fact it was worse because I was really stiff and sore. Maybe I should've gone to the gym more.

We'd moved from the potato fields to the strawberry patch. Though there was more squatting and my quads burned, at least I wasn't allergic to anything there.

"You missed the main crop," Duncan said, pulling his cap down on his head. He'd lent me one for some relief from the sun. "These are the late ones, only good for making preserves." He looked at me like he didn't know why he was telling me these things, I should know all this if I were actually from around here, but there was no way for me to hide my lack of farming skills. I just shrugged and nodded anyway.

My hands were stained red with the juice and my back ached. So did pretty much every other part of my body. I didn't know where John Lennon got off thinking strawberry fields were all romantic and poetic. He obviously hadn't spent any time picking.

After a lunch of biscuits and gravy, which I had to admit was pretty tasty, I was about to head out with Duncan when Josie showed up.

"Timothy?"

"Oh, hey, Josie."

"Are you coming to the send-off tonight?"

I shrugged. "What's the send-off?"

"It's a party at the Turners' barn. For the soldiers before they head back to camp and off to war."

"Yeah, sure. I'll come." Anything to help pass the time. Besides, Josie's cheeks were flushed from talking to me. I liked how I affected her. I smiled and her smile grew even wider.

"That's splendid. I'll leave a clean change of clothes for you on the cabin steps. You look like you'd fit into Willie's."

Clean clothes and a party? Bonus. I mentally scheduled a swim in the lake to wash up.

Josie twirled a little, the skirt of her dress flaring out, but I still couldn't get a glimpse of her legs.

"You'll dance with me, Timothy?"

"Uh, I'm not much of a dancer."

"Me either, but it doesn't look hard. We could learn together."

Why not. "Okay, sure. I have to go now, or Duncan will chew me out for talking to you."

I left with a little skip in my step. I wondered how teens partied in the nineteenth century.

8

TIM

I FOUND A SECLUDED SECTION of the lake, stripped down to my birthday suit and jumped in. The initial shock of moving from hot and sticky to cool and wet only lasted a moment and after a few minutes of kicking my legs like an eggbeater, the lake felt like a bathtub.

It was fitting since I was completely naked. I'd never skinny dipped before and it was strangely exhilarating, though I did find myself checking for stray Watson kids, or day workers wandering by.

I'd snagged the bar of soap from the cabin, a rough, harsh looking bar. Homemade, probably. Certainly no gentle dove image stamped into it. I scrubbed my skin with it and did my best to lather my hair. Anything would be an improvement. Then I dried off with a small towel. The warmth of the sun smoothed out my goosebumps. The pants Josie had left on the step for me were made of wool or something, kind of itchy with a button-up fly. The shirt was white with some sort of tie thing I didn't know how to do up.

Later, back at the cabin when it was almost time to go,

Duncan helped me to get it on right, and I was more than just a little uncomfortable with the close encounter.

Nothing against Duncan, I just preferred his sister.

The whole family piled into two carriages. I sat next to Duncan and across from Josie, who had a younger sister on her lap. I remembered what Casey had said about being alone with the opposite sex unchaperoned and it dawned on me how lucky I was that Casey had found us together in the barn and not Mr. Watson.

I had a window seat and this was my first view of the road to Boston in 1862. Let's just say it was bumpy. Not much to look at either. Mostly farms and farmhouses and lots of trees.

Sara sat squished in beside Josie, her face blotching red. "I just hate saying goodbye, especially in these circumstances," she said.

"Henry and Willie aren't leaving tonight," Josie answered. "Don't think about that. Have fun."

"Yes, you are right," she wiped her nose with a small piece of cloth. "Tomorrow has enough worries of its own."

"Who's Henry?" I said.

Sara blushed again but Josie answered, "Henry is Sara's betrothed."

Sara was engaged? I worked to keep the surprise I felt off my face. She didn't look old enough to be getting married to me.

We didn't go all the way into Boston, more like East Cambridge or somewhere in Somerville. We turned up a long drive made of two parallel grooves in the grass, and finally arrived at the Turners' barn. A load of horses and carriages filled the yard. I took a whiff. And also a lot of horse manure.

I followed Duncan into the barn, which wasn't as big as I'd imagined. I pictured something more like a hall, but it was an actual barn. No wonder there were so many horses in the yard. They'd been booted out for the evening. Open wooden beams ran up the walls and across an arched ceiling. A loft filled with hay opened up to the room on the far end with a makeshift stage set up under it.

A band consisting of four guys–a banjo, a flute, a fiddle, and a rickety looking drum–were pounding out something musical. I'd never heard music that wasn't amplified before, but they managed to be loud enough to fill the room. I noticed they favored tunes with strong patriotic themes.

Couples were already dancing in the middle of the floor, and I knew I was going to be in trouble trying to dance with Josie. I pictured the kind of dances that we had at school, where you just pressed up against a girl and swayed back and forth a little. This was an actual move your feet and the six-inch rule.

And much like a high school dance, the guys gathered in a group on one side of the building and the girls huddled together on the other side, but both sides were constantly glancing over to the other. Some things don't change, even in a hundred and fifty years.

Willie had his uniform on. The blue coat had brass buttons down the front and on the cuffs, long to mid-thigh over gray pants. He wore a blue, suede cap on his head that had two little brass muskets crossing each other on the front of it. A wide leather belt with a rectangular brass buckle was cinched at the waist.

He was talking to another guy about the same age, stocky and blond with a full beard and mustache forming, and also dressed in uniform.

"That's James Whitbey," Duncan said, following my gaze. "Willie's good friend."

"Also heading off to war," I said, stating the obvious.

"James just enlisted. His father is very much against it." Duncan sighed. "Yeah, lucky devils. They get all the fun."

I didn't remember very many details about the Civil War from my American history class, in fact, I was pretty sure I'd slept through most of it, only getting by because I sat next to Pamela Hines, who let me cheat. I did remember that the war went on for a few years.

"Don't worry, I'm sure you'll get a chance," I said.

"Perhaps. When the war started last year, everyone expected a swift victory. No one believed it would still be running through a second summer season. So, maybe you're right."

I was right. It was slightly unnerving knowing the future. Too bad I couldn't take advantage of it, like to buy stocks or something.

Not that I had money. Or knew anything about stocks.

The group of guys started thinning out as more of them made their way to the girls and asked them to dance.

Sara was dancing with some guy who must be the Henry fellow she was engaged to. I hadn't seen her in anything but a kitchen dress before, and despite my earlier judgments on her plain looks, she actually looked attractive tonight. I didn't like the big hoop thing all the women had going on, but it helped that she was smiling. Henry was on the short side with wide shoulders and dark hair parted on the side. He wasn't what modern girls would call a hottie, but you could tell by the way he was staring at Sara he thought she was something.

Duncan was watching them, too.

"You going to dance?" I said.

He shook his head. "No, I'm not, I don't, it's no..."

"Whoa, don't hurt yourself." I patted him on the back. "Someone has to keep watch over here." I looked over his shoulders and saw Josie staring our way. She was extra pretty tonight with long ringlets that hung down her back and a ribbon in her hair. I'd better get over there if I wanted to stay in her good books.

I started across the floor, and she met me in the middle, her face wearing a brilliant smile. Maybe wool pants were considered hot in the 1800s.

I offered both of my hands, hoping she'd guide me. She understood and placed my right hand on her waist and took my left hand in hers. Her other hand rested on my shoulder. A safe adult approved six inches remained between our bodies like a force field.

"I don't know what to do," I confessed.

"You never went to a dance in Springfield? Did your mother not teach you?"

"Uh, my mother wasn't well."

"It's okay, I'll lead."

I followed her footsteps, only landing on her toe once, and we managed to move in some kind of circle.

The music was loud enough that you couldn't hear the shuffling of our feet, but not so loud that we couldn't talk, unlike at home when you had to shout in your partner's ear if you wanted to say something.

Thinking of home made me a little, I don't know, homesick? A pit had grown in my gut and that surprised me. For months now all I'd wanted to do was get away from my house and my family. Here I was, independent of them, dancing with a pretty girl, and I felt a little depressed.

Josie noticed, her lips pulled down in a cute little pout. "Is everything okay, Timothy?"

"Yeah, fine." I forced a smile. "I was just wondering. How often does my sister come to work for your family?"

"Well, it's hard to say with her. She comes and goes a lot but doesn't really ever stay that long." Her eyes sparkled with a memory. "Once, there was this big scandal."

"Scandal?" That surprised me. Casey was as good as they came. She never did anything *wrong*. It wouldn't occur to me to put the words "scandal" and "Casey" in the same sentence.

"Yes," Josie's full red lips turned up. "A very wealthy man, who turned out to be a scoundrel, asked Cassandra to marry him. In front of everyone at a banquet he hosted at his mansion. Can you imagine?"

No I couldn't. "A rich guy actually proposed to my sister?"

"She never mentioned this?"

I shook my head.

"Your brother Nathaniel was very troubled by the matter."

"I bet he was." I smiled at what must've been a nasty situation for perfect Nate Mackenzie. "So what happened?"

"Cassandra said, 'Maybe.' Softly, like a little mouse. But the hall was so quiet that everyone heard her. Mr. Willingsworth's face grew red with embarrassment, but he recovered by making a joke and basically ordered everyone to get back to eating."

I chuckled. I would've liked to have seen that. What a surprise Casey had turned out to be with this secret adventurous life.

Why did all the good things always happen to her?

"When was the last time Case, uh, Cassandra came to stay with you?"

"Eight months? A year? I can't remember."

"A year?" I was stunned. I imagined being left here for a day or two, maybe a week, but a year? Suddenly my throat had grown very dry.

The song ended, and Josie led me to the refreshment table, where we were given lukewarm, sweetened tea. No ice, of course. I chugged mine back and asked for more.

In the corner a group of young guys had gathered in a crooked line up.

"What's going on over there?" I asked Josie.

"That's the recruiting table. President Lincoln has put a call out for more volunteers."

I put my empty cup on the table and started walking. A poster hung off the end of the table.

General Pope's Army

"Lynch Law for Guerrillas and No Rebel Property Guarded!"
IS THE MOTTO OF THE
Thirteenth MASSACHUSETTS REGIMENT.

This Regiment is second to none in
regard to discipline and efficiency, and is in the healthiest
and most delightful country.

Office at Coolidge House, Bowdoin Square

Capt. C. K Mudge.
LIEUT. A. D. SAWYER.

"WE'RE MAKING it easy for fellows who can't make it into Boston," the guy behind the table said when he caught my eye.

"Timothy?" Josie tugged on my sleeve. "What are you doing?"

"I'm volunteering." I just wanted one battle, then I'd sneak off and be back at the Watson farm before Casey returned. If I had to choose between weeding and shooting, I'd take shooting any day.

9

CASEY

MOM'S PANIC PEAKED at about ten o'clock that night. It started off with frantic cleaning. First, she pushed all her home decorating samples–carpets, paint chips, window blinds–into the corner of the dining room. Then we were assaulted with the loud whine of the vacuum cleaner. After that she madly scrubbed the kitchen counter tops and the window sills.

I shrugged apologetically at Nate. I hated that he had to be here to witness our family drama, but I couldn't let him out of my sight. I didn't know when the next trip would trigger, and I'd promised him I'd take him with me. I wasn't sure how that would help, though. Then I'd just have two guys to have to find and hold onto when the dizziness began, and there was always the risk that I'd leave one or both of them behind again.

I leaned into him from our spot on the couch. "You should go."

"But..."

"It's okay. I'll go to bed soon. I never travel while I'm sleeping."

Nate nodded then. I had a feeling the whole fracturing-family scene was making him uncomfortable. "I'll be over first thing in the morning. We'll find a way to trigger a trip back."

I followed Nate to the front door and kissed him good night. Then I took a deep breath, steadying myself to face whatever came next.

Mom's lips thinned into a tight line. "We need to call the police," she said.

Dad had been staring at his touch tablet, but I don't think he'd actually touched it in the last half hour. "He's only been gone a few hours," he said. "He's sixteen, not six. They're not going to take it seriously."

"But he left his car," Mom insisted. "I found his cell phone and his wallet in the glove compartment. He wouldn't go anywhere without those."

Dad rubbed his balding head and puffed loudly through his nose. "Okay, I'll call."

I felt sick. There was no way they were going to find him tonight, and probably not tomorrow or the next day either. Before too long I'd be staring at Tim's face on the back of a milk carton.

Mom sat on the couch in the living room, leaning forward over her lap. A tear escaped down her face and I offered her a tissue.

"I'm sure he's fine, Mom."

She blew her nose, her face turning an unflattering shade of red. "Yeah, then where is he?"

I sat beside her, curling my feet under me. "I don't know, but he'll come home eventually."

"I called all his friends. None of them know where he is. Or, at least that's what they're saying."

Dad interrupted. "The police are on their way."

I closed my eyes and muffled a groan. The police were going to question me. I had to get my story straight. Did any of the neighbors see me fighting with Tim at his car? I wracked my brain trying to remember. They always seemed to be out and about at the most inconvenient times. Like last year when Tim got escorted home by the police for allegedly stealing cigarettes. News of yet another family humiliation (the first being the separation of my parents), hit Facebook almost immediately. I thought of Chase Miller. Had he been loitering outside, as seemed to be his habit?

The doorbell rang, and Dad let in two police officers who introduced themselves then followed Dad into the living room.

They asked Mom and Dad a bunch of questions about Tim, and I winced when they described him as angry and rebellious. My mother broke down in tears again when she told them about finding drugs in his room.

Tim was going to be in a heap of trouble when he got back, and likely he'd be blaming me. If he hadn't gotten left in the past, the police wouldn't have been involved.

Okay, I kind of expected to be questioned but not to be treated like a suspect. Two officers stood before me. A tall one with a comb-over and a mustache, and his younger, shorter sidekick. I sat on the couch and the way they stared down at me made me feel like I was back in fifth grade hiding a wad of gum in my cheek when Mrs. Black demanded to look inside my mouth.

"When was the last time you saw your brother?" The tall one said.

I couldn't help staring at his mustache, how it looked like it was growing up his nose.

I averted my eyes. "I came home just as he was leaving."

The younger cop jotted my answer down in a notepad he'd ceremoniously flicked open.

"What were you doing just before you got home?" the first officer asked.

"Saying good -bye to my boyfriend in the front yard."

"Who's your boyfriend?"

"Nate Mackenzie." The officer with the note pad jotted his name down. I shifted nervously. I really hoped I hadn't gotten him in trouble somehow.

"Did you know your brother was doing drugs?" The mustache officer asked.

"No," I stated emphatically. "And just to be clear, there's no proof he was doing drugs."

The officer's eyebrows jumped a little, giving away his personal doubt.

"According to your mother, he was in possession."

"Well, that doesn't actually mean they were his."

My mother butted in. "Just like the cigarettes weren't his."

Please, Mom, you're not helping.

"Do you know who he got the drugs from?"

I wondered why no one had told him the mustache just wasn't working. Didn't he have a wife or a mother?

"No," I said.

"Your boyfriend maybe?"

"No!"

My strong answer made the note-taker look up.

Mustache said, "You're sure about that?"

I kept my voice steady. "Yes, I'm sure. Nate and Tim never hung out. They don't really like each other."

"Why is that?"

Oh, why did I add that last bit? These guys were making me nervous, and I wiped sweat off my top lip. I probably totally looked like I was lying. Which I was. It was a necessary evil. If I told them the truth, they'd probably lock me up.

"Miss Donovan?"

"Tim's just not that friendly. Maybe he didn't like me dating an older guy. Nate doesn't like how Tim treats the family."

"How much older is Nate?"

Oh my God, how did this get to be about Nate?

"Two years."

"Do you have an address for Mr. Mackenzie?"

"Why?" I started to freak. "This has nothing to do with him."

"We'll be the ones to determine if that's the case, miss."

I reluctantly told them his address and the note taker jotted it down. At least I knew they wouldn't find anything incriminating, but I felt bad that Nate would have to go through an uncomfortable interrogation. And I hoped he wouldn't unintentionally say anything that could complicate matters.

Like I just did.

They left saying they'd contact us the moment they had any news. I went directly up the steps to my room, with mom and dad glaring at my back. I knew they didn't believe me either.

· · ·

I WOKE the next morning to Lucinda's ring tone. I could picture her petite self pushing her long black hair–hair I'd spent most of my existence coveting–behind her ears and tucking her cell phone against the side of her face.

"Lucinda?" I said.

"I think Josh wants to break up with me."

I sat up against my pillow. "Why would you think that? I thought you were doing great?"

"I thought so, too." Her voice broke. "But he's not returning my calls or my text messages. I haven't seen him for almost a week."

"Well, he could be busy with work and stuff."

"That never stopped him before. I can just tell he's cooled off."

I studied my nails. I probably should take a file to them soon. "You're sure you're not just jumping to conclusions?"

"I don't think so. The last time we were together all he could talk about was how much he preferred the balmy weather of Florida compared to the extreme temperatures here, and how awesome UF was."

"It's natural he'd be excited about his time at college."

"Yeah, and college girls."

I bit my lip. I worried about that, too. Nate didn't leave the state, but how long before he got tired of hanging out with a high school student?

"You're as good as any college girl. Josh would be an idiot to let you go."

"You think so?"

"Of course I do. You're awesome."

"You have to say that because I'm your best friend." I heard the smile in her voice. Crisis averted.

"Anyway," she continued. "I hear your brother's up to no good again."

My jaw went slack. "Word's out already?"

"Yup, so what did he do this time? Steal a car? Mug an old woman?"

Wow, Tim's reputation was preceding him. "Actually, Mom found a suspicious substance in his room."

"No way.

"Way."

She snorted. "How long is he grounded for this time?"

"Well," I made the mistake of trying to run my fingers through my curls. "They haven't exactly found him yet."

"He's missing?"

I winced as I pulled my hand out of my knotted mess. "Sort of."

"How can you be sort of missing?" she said. I could picture her eyebrows furrowing.

"Um..."

"Casey?"

I cleared my throat. "I kind of took him back and left him there."

"Um, I'm sorry. It sounded like you said you took him *back*." She paused briefly. "And left him there."

"That *is* what I said."

Lucinda gasped. "How?"

I told her about how angry I'd gotten with him about the stash Mom had found, and about how I felt like he was wrecking our family life after it'd just had a chance to get back to normal.

"He tried to pluck my fingers off his car door, and it happened."

"And you came back *without* him?"

I sat on the edge of the bed feeling irritated. "I didn't mean to. It was his stupid fault. I told him to be ready but instead he had to make out with the first girl he saw."

Lucinda clucked on the phone. "Sounds like he deserved to be left behind."

I agreed. "The scare might do him good, but I hate what it's doing to my parents."

"So what's the plan?"

That was just it. I let out a long sigh. I didn't really have a plan.

10

TIM

TODAY WAS THE DAY. I for one was not sorry to ditch this farm. With the exception of not seeing Josie, I wouldn't care if I never stepped foot back here again.

Which I knew was impossible. I had to come back eventually to find Casey and catch my first class ticket back to the future.

The Watson house was thick with emotion now that they had to say goodbye to their golden boy again. This time he was headed to a camp to help train new recruits like me before we were all sent out to the front lines.

I really hoped that wouldn't take long. I lifted my arms like I held an imaginary rifle and shot at an imaginary foe. Pow!

I left the cabin and went looking for Josie. I wanted to make sure we had time for a private goodbye.

Willie entered the back yard as I crossed it.

"Hello, Timothy," he called, waving me over.

"Hey," I said.

Willie's ginger hair glistened in the sunlight. He'd taken

time to grease it back, and for a moment I wondered if I should've put more effort into my appearance. Joining the Union Army was a big deal.

"I've been meaning to ask you," Willie started. He ran one hand over the other and studied the ground, looking uncomfortable.

I wondered if he'd found out something about me and Josie, and if I was about to get a "talkin' to."

I pulled on the collar of my shirt. "Yeah?"

"Does your family know you've enlisted?"

Okay, so not about Josie. I let out a small breath and shrugged. "I suppose they'll find out eventually."

Willie shook his head, clearly unimpressed. "Are you sure you don't want to notify them of your plans? There will always be another call to volunteer."

"No, I want to go now. The Union needs men now."

Besides, I'd rather go with guys I sort of knew, like Willie and his friend James. If I waited, I'd be with complete strangers.

Willie's frown grew deeper. "But what about Cassandra? Would she approve?"

"She's not my mother." I said, and Willie's eyebrows shot up. I supposed that came off a little disrespectful. I softened my tone. "I mean, she would understand. She's used to me making my own decisions."

Willie's shoulders lifted as he inhaled deeply. "Very well then. We shall be leaving for camp within the hour."

He disappeared to the front of the house and I stuck my head in the kitchen hoping to find Josie. She was there, stirring something in a large bowl with a big wooden spoon. I motioned for her to meet me outside.

Sara spotted me. "Is there something you need, Timothy?" she said, wiping wet hands on her apron.

"Uh, I was looking for Willie?"

"He just went outside. You didn't see him?"

"I must have missed him. I'll go look around."

Josie removed her apron and picked up a bucket. "I'm going for water, Sara."

I moved out of her way as she pretended to ignore me. Sara's eyes were on me, and I feigned disinterest as well.

"I'll check the front of the house," I said, before leaving.

And of course, I headed straight for the water pump.

"You look so handsome, Timothy," Josie said when I joined her. She dropped her bucket on the ground and I shot her my winningest smile.

"I just wanted to say goodbye before I left."

She giggled and her dark eyes shone. I loved how her face lit up when she saw me, and I felt mine shine for her as well. I had a sudden and unexpected surge of disappointment that I wouldn't be able to see her every day any more.

I crooked my finger. "Come here."

She reached for my hand and pulled me into the cover of the forest.

"I'll miss you," she whispered, "but I'm so proud of you."

"I'll miss you too," I said, and I wasn't lying. I leaned in and kissed her cherry red lips.

"You'll stay safe," she said through our kisses.

"Of course." I was so tuned in to what was going on between us, I never heard the footsteps approaching.

"Josephine!"

We snapped apart at Sara's stern voice.

Busted.

11

CASEY

I GOT CLEANED UP and dressed quickly in denim shorts and a cotton blouse. I left my bed unmade, and my steel-blue quilt a knotted mess. My discarded clothes from the day before lay on the floor. Normally, I'd take the time to tidy things up, but not today. I stood in front of my mirror debating what to do with my hair, and settled with pulling it back into a low knot.

When I went downstairs I found my mom and dad sitting together at the kitchen table, a coffee pot and two half empty cups between them. Mom's eyes were rimmed red and dad was grasping her hand, giving it a comforting squeeze.

I cleared my throat. "G'morning." No emphasis on the "good."

"Casey come sit down," Dad said. "We want to ask you a few questions."

Didn't I get the third-degree last night? "Can I get breakfast first?"

Dad nodded, and Mom blew her nose. I gathered up a

bowl of cereal and a glass of juice before joining them. I scooped up my first bite of cereal, and the crunching of the flakes and granola filled my ears.

"Casey," my mom began, "if there's anything you're not telling us about Tim, please tell us. We promise that you won't get in trouble."

"You're not protecting him by keeping his confidences," my Dad added.

I could barely swallow my next bite. The pain on my parents' faces broke my heart.

"I wish I could help," I said shaking my head.

They stared at me stony-eyed, like they didn't believe me and hurt because they didn't understand why I wouldn't help them.

I finished breakfast, brushed my teeth and went outside to wait for Nate. Usually, I spent either the mornings or afternoons working for my mom at her interior-design business–making appointments, filing, data entry, that kind of thing–but with Tim's disappearance, she put her projects on hold. In fact, she hadn't even changed out of her pajamas.

The step was warm from the morning sun. I tilted my head and closed my eyes, letting the rays massage my face.

"Mornin', neighbor."

My eyes snapped open to see Chase Miller standing six feet away gazing at me.

For some reason the sight of him made my heart race. He just startled me that was all.

"Oh, hi," I said, feigning nonchalance.

The cuff of his T-shirt had pulled up and a black tattoo peeked out from underneath. Some kind of bird. Chase saw me gawking at it and wiped a hand to smooth out the cuff of his sleeve.

"Quite the party you had here last night," he said, distracting me. His mouth moved into a half grin that was somehow charming.

I pushed a curl off my face. "What do you mean?"

His eyebrows danced. "Do you often have cops dropping in?"

"No." I hid the discomfiture I felt knowing he'd witnessed our police visitation. "Um, my brother's missing."

Chase's flirty grin (yes, flirty!), morphed into concern. "Really? What happened?"

"Well," I stalled not knowing what the official word was. "We don't know. He may've just run off with his friends."

He tilted his head. "The rebellious type?"

My eyes found their way to his and locked on. "You could say that."

Chase's gaze never broke from mine and I couldn't stop the shiver of nerves it caused. I forced my eyes closed.

"Let me know if there's anything I can do to help," he said.

Sweet of him, but too bad there was nothing he could do. "I'll keep that in mind."

Just then Nate pulled into the drive.

"Uh, that's my ride." I stood and brushed dust off my butt. "I gotta go."

"Sure." Chase said, stepping backwards toward his house. "See you around."

Chase was gone before I could introduce him to Nate, who must've seen us talking as he drove up. His eyes narrowed as he watched Chase disappear into his yard.

"Who was that?" he said.

"New neighbor. Just being friendly."

Nate stared at the Miller house like he wasn't too crazy

about the boy next door, but I took his arm and directed us to the neighborhood park where we could talk in private.

"I have to get Tim back ASAP," I said. I didn't have time to focus on anything else, especially distracting new neighbors. "His disappearance is ripping my parents up."

"Slow down." Nate tugged on my arm. I hadn't realized I'd started speed walking. "Let's think this through."

I stopped and faced him. "You're right. We need to think. Okay, I'm thinking. Think, think think, thinking."

He took both of my arms and forced me to stare into his beautiful, bright eyes. "Breathe, Casey, it's going to be all right."

I just loved how he took charge. I suddenly wanted to kiss him.

Kiss him! That could work. I grabbed his neck and laid a good one on him. At first he stiffened in surprise, but then he relaxed into it, wrapping his arms around my waist.

I waited for the dizziness to start and held on to Nate tightly. He tried to pull back but I just kissed him harder.

"Casey." He pushed me off. "What's going on?"

My heart sank a little. "It didn't work. It used to work."

"What?" His eyes widened in question. "Kissing me?"

"Yes," I said carefully. "Well, not only kissing you, just being near you."

A shadow flitted across his face. "Are you saying I don't... affect you the same way anymore?"

I frowned. "I guess not."

I glanced at him in time to see hurt fill his eyes. "No! You do affect me, I'm still affected, very, very affected, it's just..."

"My presence doesn't shoot you off into the past anymore."

I reached for Nate's arm. "I'm comfortable with you now,

in a good way." I smiled hoping for one in return. "It'd be really inconvenient if we tripped every time we kissed. We'd be like yo-yos flying through time."

The smile I was desperate for finally appeared on Nate's face. "Good point. As long as your flame hasn't gone out."

"It's not out, I promise you."

"Good. So, anyway," Nate said as we started walking again. He threaded his fingers through mine. "I didn't get a chance to tell you that I had a little visit from your cop friends last night."

"Oh, no." I squeezed his hand. "Was it terrible? I'm so sorry."

"Relax, it was fine. I actually didn't have anything but the truth to tell. The last time I saw Tim he was walking into your house."

"I'm not a good liar. They could tell I was holding back, but it's not like I can tell them the truth."

"No you can't, so getting back to the task at hand." He ran a hand through his hair. "How about bungee jumping?"

"Bungee jumping?

"Yeah, doubles. That should get your heart pumping."

"But you do remember when we return, it's to the exact same moment when we left. All of a sudden we'd be hanging upside down over a river or something. And what about Tim? We'd drop him, and he could be killed."

"Okay, maybe not a good idea."

I didn't notice the Toyota pulling into the parking lot, but when the driver's dark head popped out, I recognized Lucinda.

"Your mom said you might be here," she said.

"Hi," I said, realizing I'd left my cell phone in my bag at

home. Then I saw her eyes, all puffy and red. "Lucinda? Are you all right?"

She burst into tears, "Josh broke up with me."

I was stunned. "Since this morning?"

"He dropped by on his way to work and said he didn't want to drag things out anymore. He met someone at UF and even though they aren't official, he didn't want to lead me on. He likes her now, not me."

She let out a huge sob, and I wrapped her in a safe, non-skin-touching hug. "Oh, Luce."

I felt badly since I was the one who'd pulled strings to get them together. Josh was a friend of Nate's, and if it weren't for me, he'd never have noticed Lucinda.

I appealed to Nate with my eyes.

"Uh, Josh is..." Nate's face flattened out. "He's just... he's not ready to..."

Lucinda drew a tissue out of her purse and blew her nose. "Thanks, you don't have to make excuses for him."

The three of us sat on a bench, with me in the middle, all of us looking kind of lost.

"I didn't mean to interrupt." Lucinda hiccuped.

"It's fine," I said, though I was starting to get antsy about sitting around and not finding a way to get back to Tim.

Nate must've felt the same way. "But we really should..." he started.

"Oh," Lucinda said, "I totally forgot about Tim. Oh my goodness, Casey, you need to get back to him. "

"The question is how," Nate said.

Lucinda wiped mascara from under her eyes with her tissue. "Have you tried making out?"

"Lucinda!" I said, my face growing crimson.

She flashed me a conflicted look. "Well, it used to work."

Nate frowned and folded his arms across his chest. "We already tried that."

Lucinda's dark eyes grew wide. "And it didn't work?"

"Lucinda, please. I need stress. Nate doesn't stress me out anymore." Though this conversation was.

"Okay, let's think," Lucinda said.

"We've ruled out bungee jumping," Nate said. Lucinda sent him a "well, duh" look.

"It's not like it's anything specific," I said. "I mean, I'm stressed out about Tim and my parents already. Why isn't it working?"

"Time travel is anything but predictable," Nate said. He got that right.

Lucinda jumped to her feet, almost knocking me off the bench. "I've got the best idea!"

12

TIM

YOU KNOW THAT "fight or flight" impulse they talk about when you're caught in a difficult or dangerous situation? It's true. I wasn't about to fight Sara Watson, so it was time to flee.

"I gotta run," I said flashing Josie a disappointed look. I really wished for a sweeter goodbye. "I don't want to miss my bus."

"Bus?" Sara said to my back as I took off.

"Bye, Timothy!" Josie called out.

I overheard Sara tear into her. "What are you thinking? Do you really want to damage your reputation this way? Timothy Donovan is nothing like his older siblings, but then again, neither are you."

Oh, harsh. I felt bad I'd put Josie in that position, but there wasn't much I could do about it now.

I made a quick stop at the cabin to grab my small bag of personal belongings (thanks mostly to Josie), and then kept going until I hit the main road in front of the house. Willie was there along with most of the Watson clan. I stayed off to the side so I wouldn't get in the way of their goodbyes, trying especially hard to be invisible when Sara and Josie finally joined us.

Willie received hugs and tears from Mrs. Watson and the girls, and handshakes from Mr. Watson and the guys. I got glaring eyes from Sara while Josie blew me a discreet kiss, and the rest gave me several pats on the back. The carriage heading for training at Camp Cameron, a rendezvous and instruction camp, stopped on the road in front of us, and Willie and I climbed on.

Willie took a seat beside James Whitbey and I sat across from them.

The carriage was pretty full and was smaller than a city bus by a long shot–shorter wooden benches, a narrower aisle with a worn wooden floor and a lower wood framed ceiling. You could tell the new recruits from the old ones by the eager and nervous looks on their faces. Those who were returning had sober expressions like they wished they hadn't gotten out of bed.

Not me. I felt like I was truly alive for the first time in my life. I knew more than most about the hardships to come, but I was up to it. I wanted to fight.

I tapped my foot and jiggled my legs, trying to release some of my nerves until Willie shot me a look of annoyance. I didn't want to get on his bad side, so I stopped.

"How long do you think we'll train at Camp Cameron?" I said to make conversation.

Willie adjusted the cap on his head. "They move the boys through fairly quickly. I'd guess only a few days."

I hoped he was right. I wanted to get out on the field before I had to head back to the Watsons to find Casey. At least for a couple days, just long enough to get a few good shots off, maybe take down a confederate or two. Then I'd sneak away. Defect. Another sort of rebellion that excited me.

The carriage turned off the main road and down a long drive through a farmer's field. The funny thing was, this was my turf in my own time. But here, I didn't recognize anything. There weren't any identifying landmarks. I had no clue where I was exactly, though I'd overheard the camp was somewhere near Somerville.

We came to a bunch of outbuildings and the horses stopped, letting out several snorts and whinnies to announce our arrival.

A blue-eyed man with a mustache and hair long enough to stick out from under his cap greeted us. He had golden buttons done up to the collar of his uniform and decorative stripes on the ridges of his shoulders that meant he was a fourth lieutenant or something. He stood with hands to his sides and though I understood he was in charge, it seemed he was just as surprised as anyone to be in his position of authority.

"Welcome, gentlemen. You are now officially part of the regiment known as the Massachusetts 13 Infantry under the command of General John Pope. You will be trained here to march and fight. The battle rages on, and you are now required by God and country to fight for the restoration of the Union." He pointed to a younger soldier dressed in the same blue and gray uniform as me. "Private Jennings will direct you to the barracks. Training begins promptly at eleven hundred hours."

Several long buildings, at least fifteen, stood side by side like gigantic loaves of bread. Private Jennings called out our names and barrack numbers, and I was relieved to be assigned the same barrack as the rest of the men on our coach. The barrack felt even longer and narrower from the inside. The wooden building had doors at both ends and bunk beds lined up along the length of both walls. The middle walkway was straight and narrow, like a long, singular bowling lane. There was room for a hundred guys, and it smelled like it. I wrinkled my nose at the lingering scent of body odor and bad breath.

These were built in a hurry. I could see daylight peeking through cracks in the wall as I picked an upper bunk near the front and climbed up. The thin mattress was hard, filled with hay or something equally unpleasant and bumpy. The blanket was rough wool, worse than the stuff my itchy pants were made of. Okay, so not the Hilton.

I studied the government-issued backpack full of goods on my bunk. I pulled out a set of the long, cotton underwear the guys around here called "drawers," a button-down shirt, a pair of wool socks and one pair of wool "trousers." Man, didn't they know it was summertime?

Over this I was to wear a boring-looking jacket and pair of tie up boots. It was topped off with a cap deep enough to gather nuts and berries. Which was why it was called a forage cap, I learned.

I put the uniform on and wished there was a mirror for me to check out my appearance. I was skeptical and suspected I'd become a nineteenth century nerd. The jacket hung loosely, and the pant legs ended at my ankles. The cap was meant for a man with a larger head than I had.

I dumped out the haversack they gave me. Lots of goodies in there. A canteen, a comb, a sewing kit, and some kind of metal kazoo looking thing. I held it to my lips and hummed out a tune. It tickled.

A small book. I picked it up and viewed the title. *The New Testament*. That was part of the Bible, right?

A pipe and tobacco. Ah, now we were talking. I imagined myself encamped around a fire, sitting back, smoking my pipe together with the other guys. Male bonding at its finest.

I stretched out on my bunk. Even though it was lumpy and uncomfortable, I liked how I could see everything in the barrack from the vantage point of my head on my pillow—with the exception of the bunk directly under me. Willie and James took the bunk opposite the bowling lane. I recognized the guy next to James. He was engaged to Sara Watson.

"Hey, Henry," I said.

Henry raised a dark eyebrow.

"It's Tim, uh, Timothy, from the Watsons. I met you at the barn dance."

"Oh, yes, of course. Hello."

Henry wasn't much into small talk. He set his belongings at the foot of his bed, then sat on the edge with folded hands.

I leaned up on one elbow and called out to Willie.

"Is it really that bad out there?" I'd heard some of the guys grumbling about the marching and waiting.

"Out where?"

"On the field, in battle?"

"I suppose it depends on what you mean by *bad*. I wasn't particularly fond of being shot at."

I harrumphed. Willie broke his arm in a fall. It wasn't like he took a bullet. "But, wasn't it exciting? The whole battle situation, I mean."

Willie raised an eyebrow and James started chuckling. "Got a live one here, Willie," he said.

Willie's face darkened. "It's not like target practice. Real people die real deaths. They go home in a box."

Eh, loosen up. I flopped down on my back and folded my arms across my chest and worked to calm my nerves. I was ready to get this party started.

The next day I was hoping to get on with target practice, but the fourth lieutenant guy made us march around a big field instead. We had to line up in long rows, with our jackets and packs on, just like if we were marching in the field. One of the lieutenant's peons would shout orders and we'd have to follow them, turning left or right, then straight or stop. Boring stuff like that. I supposed we would've looked impressive from the bleachers, if there were bleachers here. A thousand guys marching in unison like a huge band.

My head sweat under my cap and I melted under the stupid wool coat. My shoulders burned from the pack. I was more than relieved when the bugle sounded and we were dismissed for lunch.

After a so-so meal in the mess hall, a male-only version of a high school cafeteria with bad jokes and body noises, Private Jennings announced that the lieutenant was waiting for us in the armory building. Finally, we were going to be given weapons.

A musket was produced and a whistle went up in the crowd.

"Yes, men," the lieutenant said. "These are 1861 Springfields." He ran his hand along the smooth barrel. "It's thirty-eight inches long with a range of five hundred yards. Much more accurate than the 1855."

An approving murmur ran through the crowd of men as we lined up to receive our new weapons.

When he placed the musket rifle in my hands, I was like

a mother being handed her new baby. I fondled it, cradled it, adored it. *I'm holding a brand new 1861 musket rifle!* Come on!

Out in the field, we lined up twenty-five yards away from crude hand drawn man sized paper targets. Another soldier demonstrated the technique. It was a lot to remember. You had to pour the gunpowder into the musket; insert a small, papery cloth called a wadding; then add the musket ball, which you packed down with a long, thin, metal pipe called a ramrod. Then you cocked the hammer halfway, and placed a bit of dry powder called a percussion cup on the pan. Then you aimed and fired.

So, loading the gun was a hundred steps that took half a day. No wonder so many men died. You could get shot twenty times in the time it took to load one musket.

I prepared to take my first shot. I did all the steps, keenly aware that the other guys went through all the steps in half the time it took me. I eyeballed the target, my heart thudding against my ribs. When the command came, I fired. The kick-back almost threw me to the ground and the gun powder that exploded around me set me off on a sneezing fit. I'd completely missed my target, not even nicking the paper. I couldn't believe my aim was that bad.

James laughed like a hyena. "Maybe we could make a trade with the Confederates. You for an old dog or something."

Willie laughed too, but at least he tried to hold it in. "You'll get better with practice, Timothy. We all miss the first time around."

I cleaned the barrel again, and followed the steps. This time when the call came to fire, I was ready for the jerk of the gun. I held my breath until the powder disbursed. I shook my head to clear the blast wondering if I'd be deaf by the time this was over. I scanned my target, then kicked the dirt. Still a miss.

Outside of musket practice, the first day in camp was uneventful. We all had chores and I was assigned to the stable, which, funny enough, I felt quite at home in now.

The guys horsed around as we got ready for bed that night, much like we did at kids camp when I was twelve, only now we had whiskers and underarm hair. James chucked a pillow at Willie, whipping him in the face. Willie returned the pillow with an impressive throw of his own. Henry stayed to himself, reading. I recognized the book. It was identical to the one sitting in my own haversack, *The New Testament*.

I managed to get a few hours sleep amongst all the snoring and sighing from other restless sleepers, but I woke with a knot in my back where a major lump in my mattress had been.

THE NEXT DAY I watched as they put a small white tent up in front of the mess hall. A wagon was parked beside it and a civilian carried glass plates from it and into the tent.

"What's going on?" I asked Willie.

"We're getting our pictures taken."

"They have photo technology already?"

Willie squinted and said, "Excuse me?"

"I mean, they can take pictures?"

"Sure. They can take photographs outside now, too. Even though he's setting up the tent as his studio, that wagon carries all his cameras and chemicals to any spot and converts it into a dark room."

So that was how we got all those old pictures from the Civil War, courtesy of people like the man in the wagon.

Private Jennings gave us instructions on how to line up, and look serious when the photographer snapped a picture. I went along with it all and presented my most serious soldier expression.

THE LIEUTENANT ENTERED the mess hall later that day like a house on fire. "Gentlemen," he said, his eyes narrowing and his jaw tight. "I've just heard from General Major Pope. As promised, we will be joining the Mass 13th, already in Virginia. Prepare to leave for Boston in the morning."

A thrum of nervous excitement moved like a wave through the room. I felt like a giddy five-year old about to be let into the candy store. It was happening, faster than I could've hoped.

I was going to war.

13

CASEY

LUCINDA'S IDEA MADE my stomach turn, and that's why I thought it could work. It was my idea to stop by the costume shop to dress for the event first. At least I wouldn't have to worry about what I was going to be wearing once I got there.

Lucinda said she had to grab something from home and to meet her at Cambridge Common. Nate and I headed to the store.

The same lady with the deep set eyes and curly gray hair was working in the costume shop as the last time I'd been here, and I must've made an impression because she remembered me.

"Another nineteenth century party?" she said with a smile.

"It's kind of a club," I said. "We love the nineteenth century."

The lady led us to the appropriate section, pointing out the men's wardrobe to Nate. He pulled a pair of black trousers out with a matching dinner jacket and tails. "I can impersonate Robert Willingsworth."

I grimaced. "I'd rather you didn't."

In fact I still wasn't sure that Nate should come with me at all. It'd be simpler if I went alone, grabbed Tim's hand and came back, but I could tell by how earnest Nate was in selecting our costumes that his mind was set.

I chose a green dress and held it up to my chin. "What do you think?"

Then I had a flashback of the Fall Dance that had started it all. Nate had asked me to dance (even though it was only a dare) and his evil girlfriend at the time, had been wearing a dress this same color. It looked fantastic on her.

I started to put the dress back.

"It's great, Casey. You'll look beautiful as always."

"I don't know. I'm not crazy about the color."

Nate sent me a confused look. "It's not a fashion event. We're on a mission here."

I shook the memories of Jessica off. "You're right. I'll take it."

We paid for the costumes and walked out of the store wearing them, our regular clothes in a bag. The lady just smiled as we left.

My stomach started to clench as we turned off Massachusetts Avenue onto Waterhouse Street and finally into the parking lot of Cambridge Common at Harvard. There were crowds of people just as we expected, and it was especially busy since school was out for the summer and the weather had been warm and dry. Mothers were pushing children in strollers, lovers were holding hands, teenagers and college students sat on the grass in tight circles and I dreaded the thought that I might actually know someone here.

Lucinda showed up with her kitchen step stool. That's

what she had to go get? She might've needed something like that because she was so short, but I was Amazon woman. I didn't need any extra height.

"Stand on this," she said.

I shook my head. "No."

"Come on, Casey." She pressed her knuckles into hips. "It'll grab everyone's attention."

Guess what was the most common fear shared by men and women? Flying. Obviously, I was not about to catch a plane.

The number two fear?

PUBLIC SPEAKING.

Lucinda's great idea was for me to recite the Gettysburg Address in a public place. We had to memorize it in American history. I was the top of my class and still knew it by heart.

My knees were already quivering, and as I glanced around at the crowd leisurely meandering through the park, I started to feel sick.

This could work.

I was certain my skin was turning as green as my dress. "I don't think I need to stand on that."

Nate took my hand. "Just do it Casey. I'm right here. I'm with you."

I smiled weakly and climbed the step-stool. If people hadn't noticed me because of my strange attire before, they were noticing me now.

I closed my eyes, and when I felt Nate gently squeeze my hand I began. "Four score and seven years ago our fathers brought forth on this continent…" I dared to open my eyes long enough to see that people had actually stopped to watch. The teens under the trees looked at me like I was crazy. One of them let out a round of mocking laughter. I snapped my eyes shut again.

"...a new nation..."

"Speak louder," Nate said.

Why? Who cared if I was heard? That wasn't the point of this exercise, but I took a breath and practically shouted the rest.

"...conceived in liberty, and dedicated to the proposition that all men are created equal."

A small crowd had gathered and Nate encouraged me to continue. My heart pounded and I felt my hands get slippery with sweat. I felt light headed and was sure I was about to faint one way or another.

"Now we are engaged in a great Civil War, testing whether that nation, or any nation so conceived and so dedicated, can long endure. We are met on a great battlefield of that war."

I felt dizzy and giddy, and that light was forming at my peripheral. It was happening! I glanced, wide eyed at Nate.

And pulled my hand free just in time.

14

CASEY

I WAS BACK and without Nate. He was going to be so mad when he realized what had happened, but by then I would already be back with Tim. No harm no foul.

I hadn't considered how Tim's sudden appearance at Cambridge Common would affect the crowd, but I decided we'd just have to dash out as fast as we could before we were riddled with questions.

The Harvard College grounds were sparse compared to its modern counterpart, like a giant hand had plucked away all the newer complexes leaving only the oldest buildings behind. I spotted the three-story, red-brick Massachusetts Hall in the distance.

Another apparent change was the number of students who meandered the paths in the summer months. Not many, and all male. I picked up my skirts and kept to the least populated paths.

My dress was a little too tight around the armpits and I pulled down on the bodice to no avail. Despite the discomfort I was thankful to already be dressed–it saved time.

My heart pumped with anxiety. I wouldn't breathe properly until I had Tim in my sights. Then I might kill him. If he'd taken this more seriously and not picked up the first girl he spotted, we wouldn't be in this situation. As it was, I could only imagine the trouble he could've gotten into since I'd been gone. I hoped he hadn't done something stupid and gotten kicked off the farm.

My brow was sweating in an unflattering fashion when I finally turned down the Watson drive. The younger kids were running around in the front yard, and they waved when they saw me.

"Hi!" One of the little boys called.

"Hi, "I called back.

I headed straight for the kitchen door, and tapped lightly before walking in. "Sara?"

She had two fists in a large bowl filled with dough, kneading it with a masterful rhythm. She stopped when she saw me. "Cassandra."

Her expression scared me. Her head tilted to the left and her mouth went soft. Her eyes looked like they were tearing up.

"What's wrong?" My heart took flight. "Did something happen to Timothy?"

"They've left." She continued her kneading. "I'm sorry I have to finish this."

I was gripped with apprehension.

"Who left?"

"Willie, Henry and Timothy."

My mouth was so dry, I could barely swallow. A memory flashed of Tim when we first arrived here, and how he brashly called out to a passing group of soldiers.

"How long ago?"

"Two days. They're not far away, though, only at Camp Cameron."

Camp Cameron, eventually Camp Day, was on the Cambridge/Somerville border. Not walking distance, but an easy day's horseback ride.

If I didn't get lost.

"I need to find him, Sara. I need to take him home."

She looked at me with pity. "We tried to talk him into going back to Springfield, tried to convince him that he should talk to his family first or to you, but he refused. He's enlisted now. They won't let him leave until his tour of duty is up."

My legs felt numb, and I slid into a chair. The enlistment tours were for three years. I knew this from my studies. My brother was an idiot!

Josephine walked into the room and Sara told her to get me a glass of water.

"Your brother is so brave," she said to me as she passed me the glass.

You mean so stupid, I thought as I gulped the water down.

It was unnerving the way Sara stared at me, but I was more than a mystery to her. I had to give her credit. She'd tired of asking me questions I couldn't answer long ago, but she still remained patient enough to allow my habitual returns. Now I wished I'd brought Nate along after all. He'd know what to do. Oh, why did I pull my hand away?

I didn't want to do anything to ruin Sara's trust, but I knew I had to do something illegal now in order to get Timothy back.

"Sara," I began, "I'm not feeling well today. Would you

mind if I retired to the cabin and returned later this evening?"

I must've looked like crap because she didn't skip a beat before saying, "Yes, by all means."

A seed of an idea began to brew in my head, but I needed help to execute it. I motioned for Josephine to follow me.

I walked toward the cabin and when I was certain we were out of earshot of the kitchen I asked, "Can you ride a horse?"

"Of course."

"Would you be free to go riding with me today?"

"I thought you weren't feeling well?"

"Perhaps a ride will brighten my spirits," I said. Then I turned to face her. "Can you keep a secret, Josephine?"

By the way Josephine's young face brightened, you would think nothing interesting ever happened to her. "I excel at keeping confidences."

Perfect. "I need to find my brother. Do you know the way to Camp Cameron?"

"We pass it weekly on our way to church."

"Can you lead me there?"

Josephine considered my request. "I suppose, but I don't think they will let us on the grounds."

"Let me worry about that. It's just it's very important that I find him."

"Is he in trouble?"

Tim was always in trouble. I nodded and showed her my sad face. "I'm asking for your help because I believe that you've developed an affection for my brother?"

I left it as a question, but if she wanted to dispute it, she didn't.

Her mouth formed a sly grin. "Perhaps."

"Okay. We must prepare two horses, and exit the farm stealthily."

Josephine let out a little giggle. "There is a path that leads out from behind the barn to a back road. It's very secluded."

"Perfect."

THE SUMMER BREEZE BLEW GENTLY; cool enough to counteract the humidity. If it weren't for the fact that I'd basically manipulated a minor into helping me find Camp Cameron so that I could break the law, it'd be just another lovely day for a ride.

I pulled up on my skirt a little more to get a firm grip with my shoes in the stirrups. They weren't custom made for the nineteenth century, unfortunately. I wore a pair of strap on sandals from a twenty-first century Wal-Mart.

Josephine stared, but there was no way I could conceal them. "Those are odd shoes," she said.

"Um, my, uh, uncle, is a shoemaker. He made these on a lark, when I told him my feet were too hot."

"Not a bad idea."

Josephine took a sip of water from the leather canteen she thought to bring along and then offered it to me.

"So, Cassandra, why do you and sometimes a brother, keep coming to our place?"

I wiped my mouth and handed the canteen back to her. "Well, like I've said before, we've a large family. Sometimes we're out of work."

"But with the war on every city is bustling. I heard Papa talking about the ammunitions factory built a year ago in

Springfield. Surely there must be enough work for everyone now?"

Who knew? I'd never been to Springfield, in this time or my own. The best tactic I'd learned in these awkward situations was to deflect.

"Are you sick of us?" I cocked an eyebrow. "You seemed pretty happy to meet my brother."

"Oh, it's not that. It's just your family is a curiosity. And I admit that your brother Timothy has a certain charm."

I wasn't used to riding, and my butt was getting sore. Nellie's tail kept swatting at annoying flies, and lifting on occasion to do her business, a procedure that didn't require stopping or slowing down. A sweaty horse smell wafted up in the heat.

We eventually came upon the farm where the army trained. I instructed Josephine to canter by as I assessed the situation. A soldier manned the entrance, and even from my vantage point on the road, I could tell he was not much older than me. A meagee fence ran roadside, nothing that would keep a man from leaving if he wanted to. But it was fairly bare of trees and bushes, so I could easily be spotted if I just walked in from the road. The entrance followed the edges of a treed area. I had to go in on that side, if I wanted to stay concealed.

"What means of escape do you have in mind?" Josephine said.

"Well, I thought you might use your female gift of persuasion as a distraction." I felt a little bad at this suggestion, but it wasn't like she had to get off her horse. Besides, the boy at the gate looked harmless.

Josephine spotted the soldier and grinned. "That sounds like fun." Then she stared at me. "What are you going to do?"

"If I can sneak by him, I can gain access to the forest immediately. When he's completely enamored by you, which will take all of two seconds, I'm going to slip past him. Once I'm in, you can go home." I patted the flank of my horse. "Nellie can carry me and Timothy back."

When we were out of the soldier's line of sight, we stopped and I slid off Nellie and tied her to the fence. "Josephine, if for some reason, we don't come back tonight, you'll need to come for Nellie tomorrow."

She stared down at me. "Why wouldn't you come back?"

"I don't know." I shrugged like it wasn't important. "You never know how things will play out."

"Are you sure you want to do this? I can attest to the fact that Timothy was eager to enlist. He was in no way coerced."

"I believe you. There are things you don't know about my brother, and you have to trust me that what I'm doing is in his best interest."

She nodded, then nudged her horse with her knees and turned him around. "Hopefully we'll see each other again later." She clicked her tongue and galloped away.

I followed on foot, watching from the bushes in the ditch as she approached the soldier at the gate. In no time flat she was giggling and the boy was staring up at her with a docile grin. I stepped carefully behind him, and would've been caught if Josephine hadn't executed a perfectly timed sneeze.

Once inside the gate, I took cover behind the trees and bushes making my way toward several rows of long narrow buildings. I was careful to stay in the shadows and out of sight.

There were a lot of men, more than I imagined, milling about. Some running a track, other's shooting off rifles on the other side of a field. Others were doing foxhole maneuvers of some kind. I peeked inside a barracks window, and saw rows of empty but made-up bunk-beds. Tim was sure to come back to this place at some point. I'd just wait it out.

I was a little worried I'd never spot him in this crowd of men, but an hour or so later I saw him coming from a large building, probably the mess hall. Unfortunately, he was with Willie and another stocky soldier with blond hair. The barrack furthest away was up against a grove of trees and bushes, and I kept myself hidden. I whistled a bird call to draw his attention. He looked my way, but didn't falter. I whistled again and this time he stopped. Willie paused, too, but the other guy kept going. Tim shrugged and started after Willie who was now a few steps ahead. I whistled again just as Willie stepped inside. Tim looked my direction; I stuck out my arm and waved him over.

"Who's there?" he said.

I popped my head out from behind the shrub. "It's me."

"Casey?"

"Yes, get over here."

Tim looked over his shoulder before ducking in behind the barracks.

"How did you get in here?" he whispered.

"It doesn't matter. We just need to wait until it's darker, and then we can sneak back out."

Tim huffed. "I'm not leaving."

"Are you crazy? You can't be here. They'll send you off to battle!" I spoke as sternly as I could in a whisper.

"I want to go to battle. It's an adventure."

"It's not an adventure. It's suicide."

"Oh, come on. You said yourself that you couldn't have died here since you're still there."

"That's just a theory. I also said I wouldn't purposely try to get myself killed."

"I'm not trying to get myself killed. I'm getting an education. This is a once in a lifetime opportunity. Who gets to experience firsthand, historical events that happened before they were born?"

"Some things are better learned from a book. I'm not arguing with you, Tim. You need me to get back." I stared hard at him. "Unless you want to stay here forever."

He scoffed. "You'll come again. I'll catch the ride back to the future next time."

So, not going to happen. I stomped my feet blowing hot air out my nose like a bull. Here I went to all this trouble to find Tim, recited the Gettysburg Address in public dressed like a dork, enlisted a minor to commit a crime, committed the crime, and now he wouldn't come with me?

A branch cracked under someone's weight and I dropped to the ground.

"Cassandra?"

Crap. Willie saw me. I stood with my finger to my mouth. Last thing I needed was to attract the attention of the whole regiment.

"I'm just here for Timothy," I said quietly.

"I don't want to go," Tim said

"Willie, talk sense to him."

Instead of taking my side, he said, "How did you get in here?"

"It doesn't matter." Was I the only sane one? Why were they wasting my time? "I'm here to take Tim home."

Willie sighed. "He's enlisted. They won't let him go."

I felt like stomping my feet like a child. "I don't care."

I zeroed in on Tim. "You are coming back to the Watson farm with me tonight."

Tim crossed his arms. "No I'm not. Now if you'll excuse me."

"You are not excused!"

Tim just smirked. "I hope you can find your way out without being caught. I'll deny knowing you if you are."

I'd run out of time trying to make him come to his senses. I felt the dizziness start. Oh, no, and with Willie standing right there.

"Would you give us a moment?" My voice was tight and I reached for my throat with my hand.

"Are you alright?" Willie said. He stepped closer instead of leaving.

"Please, Willie."

I didn't have a choice. Tim and I were going to disappear before Willie's eyes, but I couldn't risk leaving Tim here.

I grabbed Tim's hand.

But he did to me what I'd done to Nate and tugged it loose just before I disappeared. For the second time, I left my brother behind.

But I wasn't alone.

15

CASEY

I'D STARTED TO FALL when Tim pulled his hand away, and another hand grabbed mine. Moments later I was looking at Willie's wild-eyed face and I started screaming.

I was back at Cambridge Commons standing on the step stool with Willie beside me, his hand in mine. He wore his Union uniform, with his army cap sitting at an angle on his red head. The crowd started clapping and I heard people saying "How'd they do that?" Even the gawking teens looked impressed.

Lucinda's arms dropped to her sides, her jaw slack.

And Nate glared, his eyes darting from me to Willie and back.

I stepped off the stool and reached for him. "I'm sorry."

"You did that on purpose."

"I thought it would be easier if I only had to worry about bringing one person back."

"Looks to me like you brought the wrong person." He clenched his teeth and a ripple of fear dripped down my back.

Then he turned to Willie and shook his hand. "Welcome to the twenty-first century."

Nate might as well have pulled a gun on Willie, that's how frightened he looked.

The crowds returned to their nattering as if they were totally used to people appearing out of thin air and acting oddly in public places.

"Let's get out of here," Lucinda said, picking up the stool. Then to me she whispered, "Well, at least he's cute."

Willie gulped "Did he say the *twenty-first*?"

I gave him an apologetic look then ran after Nate, who walked briskly, keeping a full pace ahead of my stride. "Nate?"

"You could've told me how you felt." He stopped abruptly to face me and let out a frustrated breath. "So, where is Tim, then?"

"He wouldn't come with me!" I let my voice go all whiny.

I'd never seen Nate angry before. Frustrated, yes, exasperated, yes, but not truly angry about something I'd done.

It scared me a little.

He spun away and I turned back to find Willie slumped to the ground. Lucinda waited next to him, looking unsure about what to do.

"Willie." I rushed to his side and pulled him to his feet. I didn't miss the strange stares and the rising curiosity of the crowd around us.

"It's going to be okay," I said, trying to sound soothing. "But we have to go."

Willie scanned our surroundings as we marched through the park. The way people dressed or barely dressed. It was a twenty-first century summer, and Willie was seeing more skin than he'd ever seen in his life. The buildings towered over us, and I imagined the traffic noise must've been almost deafening to someone from 1862 who'd never seen a motorized vehicle.

He looked shell shocked, like he'd just survived a bad accident or witnessed a tragic event.

"I'm sorry, Willie," I said. "I never meant for this to happen."

"What *is* happening? What is this?" His face was filled with horror.

"This is the future," I said. How could I explain this without sounding completely insane? "I'm a time traveler. I don't know why and I don't know how. I only know that I'm on a loop between my time and yours."

"A time traveler?" he sputtered, shaking his head.

"It's weird, I know, but I move through time. Yours and mine." I held my hands together, three inches apart so that they made parallel lines. I wiggled my left hand. "Your time." Then my right hand. "My time. For some reason I jump back and forth between the two of them."

Willie wrinkled his forehead. "That's why you're always disappearing?"

"Yes. And if someone is touching me, skin to skin, when it happens, they travel with me." I paused, wishing I could unwind the last twenty minutes. "It was supposed to be Tim not you."

"He's from here?" He took in the crowds that surrounded us. "That explains his odd behavior."

I nodded my head. "He's trouble."

"Are you sure I'm not dreaming?" He squeezed his eyes shut and pinched the bridge of his nose. "Maybe I'm having a fantastic lucid dream."

I patted his shoulder. "I wish."

Just as we arrived at the spot where Lucinda's car sat, a group of teen guys rushed across the street. I recognized the buzz cut of the ginger-headed one.

Lucinda collapsed into a squat out of sight. "It's Josh."

I shrunk down beside her, not wanting to be seen dressed like a geek.

And, of course, to be a supportive friend.

Willie dropped down too, probably thinking this was normal behavior in the future. Or maybe he just felt light-headed. I wouldn't blame him.

Only Nate remained standing, though I didn't think he'd be too crazy about getting caught dressed the way he was, either.

"Did he see us?" Lucinda squeaked.

"I don't think so," I said.

She peeked around the bumper of her car. Josh and a couple guys I didn't recognize, maybe new friends who also went to UF, sauntered by, laughing and joking like they didn't have a care in the world.

I hated them.

Lucinda dropped onto her butt, and let out a slow, soft groan. "I still can't believe it's over."

"Well, maybe it's for the best," I said in my most comforting voice. "He wasn't really there for you anyway."

Lucinda sniffed into a tissue she'd plucked from a pocket in her shorts. "No, he wasn't, was he?"

"You can do better than him."

"Oh, it just hurts so much." She leaned into my shoulder and cried. I patted her on the back while Nate stood with his arms folded, leaning against the car. His eyes narrowed as he shot irritated glances our way. He wasn't hiding the fact that he'd rather be anyplace but here.

Lucinda hiccuped, and put on a brave face. "Sorry for the public breakdown."

"No problem. But Nate and I need our clothes now."

Lucinda got to her feet. "Yeah, sorry." She unlocked her car so that Nate and I could get our real clothes. I hated leaving her with nothing but a wet tissue, but I really couldn't wait to step into the public restroom and change out of this stiff dress.

She climbed into the driver's seat and I opened the passenger door for Willie. "Hop in. Just think of it as a carriage without horses. By the way," I waved over to Lucinda, "this is Lucinda. She knows about my 'gift,' if you have any questions."

Which I was one hundred percent sure he had. He cautiously scrutinized every bit of the door before getting in.

Nate was already half way to the restrooms. "Nate?" I called, my voice thin and cracking. *I'm sorry.*

He flicked a hand up in my direction. "Not now."

I'd really ticked him off, and I wasn't sure how to go about making nice. I did regret not taking him. Maybe he could've talked some sense into Tim, or even forced him to hang onto me.

As it was, my brother was to remain a missing person.

I stepped inside a stall to change. My long arms managed to undo the zipper at the back, a sure giveaway I was wearing a costume and not the real thing as zippers weren't invented in 1862, and I let it fall to my feet. It was such a relief to get back into my shorts and blouse.

Nate was already sitting in the back seat of Lucinda's car by the time I joined them. I climbed in beside him, super aware of the frosty wall that had sprung up between us.

Lucinda's eyes were still a little red, but at least she wasn't crying anymore. In fact, she and Willie seemed to be very friendly. Lucinda was in the middle of explaining how a car engine worked, and I was impressed. I didn't know she knew that much about mechanics.

"Home, James," I said lightly as if Lucinda was our chauffeur. I'd hoped to lift the heaviness in the car, but it was to no avail. With Lucinda's heartache, Willie's freaked out bewilderment, and Nate's anger, I could barely breathe.

Lucinda pulled into traffic and drove us back to the park by my house. She turned off the ignition, and we all sat there, quiet. Our arms were crooked at the elbows, and each of us leaned out of our windows. A slight breeze edged in on the muggy air.

Finally, Nate spoke. "Willie can come home with me for now. My brother's room is free."

Willie swiveled to look at me. "You'll be able to get me back, won't you?"

"Sure," I said with too much enthusiasm.

All I had to do was make sure Willie was touching me next time I traveled, even though I don't get hardly any warning going from the present to the past. No problem.

"I need to get home," Lucinda said, nudging us to get out.

Nate and I grabbed our costumes and climbed out along with Willie.

"Thanks, Lucinda," I said.

"Sure thing," she said back. Then to Willie, "Bye, nice to meet you."

Was it my imagination, or did she and Willie keep eye contact for a little longer than necessary?

I thought Nate would grab Willie, march back to his car and hightail it away from me. Instead he sat on a nearby bench. Willie wandered around staring at the houses in the neighborhood across from the park, taking in the cars that slowed as they passed, the kids riding on bikes and playing in the colorful, high-concept fiberglass playground. An airplane flew overhead on its way to Logan Airport and Willie dropped to the lawn like a rock.

I ran to his side. "It's okay."

He panted. "What was that?"

"It's called an airplane."

"What *is* it?"

"It's a mechanical vehicle, like Lucinda's car, except it can fly."

"There are *people* in it?"

I nodded. "It sounds crazy, but it's scientifically sound."

Willie shut his eyes and blew heavy breaths into the grass. I hoped he wasn't about to hyperventilate.

"Sit up and put your head between your knees," I said. He did it without question. "Now breathe into your hands."

After a few moments, his breaths slowed to a more normal state. "This is so fantastical," he croaked out.

"It's a lot to take in at once, and well, there's a lot more out there than you've seen so far." I thought it best to give him fair warning. "But you'll be okay, and I'll get you home." Somehow.

Once Willie looked like he'd survive, at least for a while, I went back to Nate.

"Is he okay?" Nate said.

"For now."

"This must be super crazy for him. I bet he's really happy he knows you."

I felt slapped. "What's that supposed to mean?"

Nate shrugged and crossed his arms over his chest. "So, what happened to Tim? Why is Willie here instead?"

I slipped onto the bench beside him, exhausted. The last thing I wanted to do was fight with Nate. All I wanted to do was go home to bed, but I could see by his frown that he'd have none of that. Plus I knew I looked like crap. I always came back with raccoon eyes, black like I'd run into a door. Twice. Best to just get this over with.

"Tim enlisted in the army."

"What?"

"He thinks it's some big adventure. When we first went back, he asked all the same kinds of questions you had, like was I afraid of changing history or afraid of dying there. I made the mistake of telling him my theory that I couldn't have died there, since I was still here. Now he thinks he's invincible or something."

"Oh, man."

"He's acting like he's on some kind of field trip." I mimicked Tim while finger quoting, "'A once in a lifetime educational experience.' But I don't know if my theory is sound. Not for sure. And even if he doesn't die there, he could get hurt."

A yawn overtook my face and my hand flew to cover my gaping mouth. "Anyway," I continued, "Josephine and I rode to the camp where his regiment is training, and I sneaked in..."

Nate's eyes snapped wide. "You sneaked in?"

"Yeah, Josephine distracted the soldier guarding the entrance."

Nate pinched his eyes together. "That sounds dangerous."

"He was just a kid. I could've taken him," I joked, but Nate didn't laugh.

"I found Tim by the barracks, erroneously assuming he

was of sound mind and would like to come back to his own time, but no. He fought me on it. We had to talk in this forced whisper; I was constantly worried I'd get caught. The more he resisted the angrier I got.

"Then Willie appeared. The trip had already triggered, so I grabbed Tim's hand. But he pulled it away, pulling me off balance in the process. Willie only thought he was keeping me from hitting the dirt when he caught my arm. That's how come he's here and not Tim."

Nate let out a low whistle. "That sucks."

I stood hiding another wide yawn with my hand. "I have to go home."

"Sure," Nate said. I waited for him to stand, too, expecting him to walk me back to my house where his car was. Instead he motioned toward Willie.

"I'll take care of our accidental tourist."

I swallowed the lump that had formed in my throat. "Okay. Thanks. Call me later?"

"Yeah."

He turned his back on me to fetch Willie. No hug or kiss goodbye. I'd really blown it this time.

In five minutes I was home, but before I reached my front door I was stopped by Chase, who waved a hose in my direction. He was washing a car, and his T-shirt was soaked and clinging to his chest in a way that wasn't at all unflattering. His long jeans covered bare feet.

"Hey," I said. I imagined it sucked being new in the summer, when you didn't have much chance to meet people. I was tired, but I didn't want to seem unfriendly. "Who's winning?"

He laughed and turned the nozzle on the hose off. "It is, I think."

"Nice car." Up close I could see it was an older model Mustang, in good shape. "Is it yours?"

His lips turned up into a crooked grin. "Yup,"

Wow, nice wheels for a teenager.

"Gift from your parents?"

"Nope. I had a job in New York."

He dried his hands on a towel and strolled over, capping his eyes from the sun "No boyfriend?" he said, nodding to Nate's car.

"Oh, he's coming later."

"Hey, wait a minute." Chase leaned toward me and peered deeply into my eyes, and I noticed how blue his were, like the sky on a sunny day. "Did he hit you?"

Right, my raccoon eyes. I stepped back and cupped my eyes like the sun suddenly got too bright. "No, of course not. He's not like that."

Chase folded his arms across his chest. "That's what they all say."

"All who?"

"Women who are abused. They never blame the guy."

"He didn't do anything. I'm just tired."

"Okay. But if you need someone..." he punched one hand with his other fist. "I'll take him out for you."

It was shocking yet sweet, how he so willingly came to my defense. "Thanks, Chase, but I'll be fine."

"If you say so."

I said goodbye and headed for the front door. I sneaked a look back as I went in. Chase Miller hadn't taken his eyes off me.

16

TIM

I'D SCREWED UP. Worse than my other screw ups. Way worse. I almost had a coronary watching Casey *and* Willie disappear before my eyes.

I actually felt sick, and jogged to the latrine.

Willie was gone. *Willie was gone!*

I brushed past James and headed for the first stall. A disgusting noise erupted from my throat that accompanied an upheaval into one of the toilets, a smelly hole in the ground that didn't help my nausea *at all*.

"Everything all right, Timothy? James asked. "Meals here aren't fit for my dog. I feel like vomiting myself."

"Uh, yeah," I mumbled as I wiped my mouth with the back of my hand. "Stomach's off."

"Hope you're not contagious. Last thing this regiment needs, now that we're shipping out in the morning."

The pit in my gut sunk deeper. I had a strong suspicion Willie wouldn't be back that soon.

I joined James at the mirrors. Other men were waiting in

line, ribbing each other. I poured water over my hands into a bowl, then splashed my face.

I had an idea to sow a seed for Willie's story.

"You know, I heard Willie saying something about feeling sick."

James shook his head. "I hope not. Disease is a bigger threat to an army than guns."

He left and another guy nudged me.

"You done?"

I grunted and left for the barracks, where I climbed on my bunk and collapsed flat on my back. Why did Willie have to interfere? Why couldn't he just mind his own business?

I tilted my head slightly until my sight lined up with Willie's bunk. It was perfectly made with his knapsack and haversack sitting upright at the foot.

A groan escaped my lips. How would I explain his disappearance when he didn't take anything with him? I considered the possibility of hiding it, but where? Then Willie would be accused of desertion, and he wouldn't thank me for it when he got back.

James had already bedded down. Henry and Joseph entered along with most of the other guys. Henry had this night time ritual that consisted of reading from his little New Testament. When he shut the book his eyes would close and his lips would move. I hoped he was praying for Willie right now.

I could use a little help myself.

Joseph, on the other hand, seemed afraid to close his eyes. I wondered if he was scared of the dark. It was his reluctance to sleep that kept him awake long enough to notice that Willie hadn't yet joined us.

"Anyone know where Willie is?" he asked softly to no one in particular.

"Uh, no," I said.

"Last I saw him was at the mess hall," Henry muttered

James moaned. "He's a big boy. He can find his way to his own bed, now if you don't mind shutting it."

Candle flames were blown out up and down the aisle and the sounds of snoring followed shortly after. My stomach twisted and turned and my chest felt like something big was sitting on it. Come sunrise, everyone would know that Willie was a no-show.

It wasn't going to be pretty.

I AWOKE TO THE BUZZ.

"Watson's defected."

"Are you sure?"

"Coward."

I pulled on my trousers and shirt. "He was sick yesterday," I said to whoever could hear me. "Maybe he's in the medical shed?"

I got a strange look from a tall, slender guy with a toothy mouth. "No, I heard they checked there already." He combed his hair, parting it on the side. "A soldier noticed the cot hadn't been slept in last night and reported it to the lieutenant."

James sat next to Henry on Henry`s bunk and they talked in hushed tones.

"This is so unlike him," James's rough voice reached me. "He didn't act like he wanted to leave. He would've told me. And even if he slipped away for the night, he would've come back."

Some guys did that, took off for the night and returned before the bugle blew. The camp wasn't fenced, and the higher-ups often turned a blind eye as long as the soldier was back for roll call.

Which Willie had missed.

"Is it possible there could be foul play?" Henry countered.

"I suppose," James said. "But who? And why?"

By midmorning, the grounds had been scoured. I was paired with Joseph to search for any sign of Willie. If he were sick or dead anywhere on the camp grounds, the lieutenant wanted to know.

Joseph looked a little pale. "I'm really not that great with blood."

I stopped to stare at him. "You're afraid of blood and you joined the army?"

"I'm not afraid of blood. I just don't like it. Rather it doesn't like me."

"Don't tell me you faint at the sight of blood?"

"I can't help it. And my father made me."

I shook my head. The kid's old man made him join the army when he was so obviously not the tough guy sort. Made me want to punch his dad in the face.

"So, what's your plan for when we fight the Confederates?" I asked. The kid wasn't going to last two minutes.

"I've joined the military band. Bugle player. I don't have to fight and I'll be fine as long as I keep my eyes closed."

Sure, he'd be fine. He wouldn't faint from the bloodshed, but he'd be a perfect blind target.

I pushed through a tangled brush. "Well, I don't think you have to worry about finding anything gruesome today."

By noon, Henry, James, and I were in the lieutenant's office getting the third degree.

His office was small and dusty and with the three of us, plus the lieutenant and his main officer, it felt like we'd squished into a broom closet.

The lieutenant's mustache wiggled as he addressed us in his stiff, low voice.

"Desertion is a federal offense with severe consequences. Hiding your friend's whereabouts is not helpful to him. In fact, if you deliver him to us today, I can guarantee a lesser charge and consequence."

James shifted under his gaze. "I swear I don't know what happened to him."

I decided to stick with my mantra. "He was sick. Maybe in his delusional state, he wandered off?"

The lieutenant lowered his bushy eyebrows at me. I didn't think he bought my line.

Henry spoke up. "As we said before, this is so unlike what we know of his character. We can't imagine what's happened to him, and we wish him found as much as you do."

The lieutenant leaned back in his chair, and slipped a pipe between dry lips. He lit it slowly making a huge show of blowing smoke rings into the air.

"I hope you're right, Private Abernathy."

He stared us all in the eyes one by one as smoke from his pipe billowed up to the ceiling of the closet-sized room.

"Because, mark my words," he finally said. "We will find him."

I kept my face like stone but scoffed in my head. *Oh, no, you won't.*

Half way back to the barracks, James muttered, "Stupid plebeian."

"Now, now," Henry said. "You know rank isn't determined by social class in the army."

"Do you see how pompous he was?" James spat. "When the war is over, he'll have to tip his hat to me."

"Soon enough," Henry said, patting him on the back. "But for now, we must remember our place."

The bell rang for dinner, the last one for us at Camp Cameron. Tomorrow we headed for Boston and then to Virginia.

I for one was ready to get a move on.

17

CASEY

WHEN I WOKE UP it was still dark. I fumbled for my phone to check the time, 5:15. I texted Nate wanting to make sure he got it as soon as he woke up. *How are you? Is Willie okay?*

I tucked my covers under my chin and stared at the ceiling. I tried to imagine what Willie must be going through right now. Freaking, that's what. I hoped at least he slept well. Today wouldn't be an easy day for him.

The darkness gradually turned to a dull gray and then a warm yellow as the sun rose, casting weird shadows against the walls. My cell buzzed just after 6:00.

"Hello?" I said.

"Hey."

Hearing Nate's voice was a balm. I immediately felt calmer, knowing that he was there for me.

"How's it going?"

"I lent him a pair of jeans and a T-shirt. He's currently playing with the zipper. He's easily entertained."

"I'm coming over." I threw off my blanket as I spoke, swinging my legs to the floor.

"Sure. I'll make pancakes. The boy looks hungry." It was a pleasant invitation, but Nate's usual lightness was missing.

I chose a pair of Capris and a red tank top. I took a little extra time with my looks, needing every advantage to get back on Nate's good side and regain his trust. I brushed out my curls and pulled my hair back with a tie, pinning up a few fly-away strands with Bobby pins. I added a light brush of mineral foundation to my face, a couple strokes of mascara to my eyes and clear gloss on my lips. I examined my reflection in the mirror. Better.

Mom was already up when I entered the kitchen. She sat at the table with a coffee, her laptop and her phone, doing whatever she could to try to locate Tim. I felt so sad for her.

"Mom?" I said, wishing there was a way I could comfort her. "He's going to come home."

Mom's eyes watered and her face turned a blotchy red. Her spiky blond hair could use a wash, but I wasn't about to say anything about her appearance right now. I wrapped my arms around her shoulders and squeezed.

"Thanks," she said "I'm keeping the faith, too. My son will come back to me."

"I'm going to Nate's for breakfast," I said as I headed to the door.

"What about work? There's a pile of papers you could scan and file on my desk."

"I know, and I'll get to it, it's just... Nate made pancakes."

She nodded and waved me off, too pre-occupied with her thoughts to question why I was heading out so early.

I CAME to a full stop when I got to the driveway. How was I going to get to Nate's? I stared at Tim's car sitting exactly where he'd last parked it and wished I could drive. I usually got shuttled around by Lucinda, my parents, Nate and sometimes Tim. Either that or I walked or caught the bus.

Nate hadn't offered to come for me like he usually did, and it was too far to walk. My dad had an early commute and was already gone, and I didn't want to bother my mother.

I glanced over at Chase's driveway, halfway hoping he'd be out and would offer me a ride, but it was too early in the morning for that. I could take the bus, but that took forever. I fished my cell out of my bag and called a taxi.

Willie was in the front yard of Nate's house when I pulled up in the yellow cab. I paid the driver and got out.

"Good morning," I said.

He nodded. "I suppose."

I recognized Nate's clothes and couldn't help but smile a little. Willie looked kind of hot.

"What are you doing?" I asked him.

"Do you see all these wires?" Willie motioned overhead. "Every house has them and they're all hooked up together to bring the magic lights. Amazing."

I tried to envision what it would be like taking in all the technology of modern times in one sitting.

"Nathaniel took a bar of butter out of a big steel box, and it was frozen solid! Then he put it into another smaller box and it thawed in less than a minute! I just can't believe what I'm seeing."

I hoped Nate hadn't showed him his laptop or iPod yet.

"It's a lot to take in, I know."

"I can't imagine what you must think of our humble home?"

The Watson house was very impressive for its day, but compared to a modern home...

"I love your home, and your family," I said. "You've been nothing but good and kind to me, letting me come and go, and infringe on your hospitality, without question."

"Well, I'm glad of it now. It must be very difficult for you. How does it work, this time travel thing?"

"I don't know. It's just a 'gift' I have. I can't control it, and I don't really understand it. I do know that I'm not the only one."

Willie raised an eyebrow. "Anyone I know?"

I cracked a smile, feeling somewhat conspiratorial. "Samuel."

Willie's brown eyes widened. "Our Samuel?"

I laughed a little and nodded. Like me, Samuel often found refuge at the Watson farm, but everyone thought he was a slave fleeing the south instead of a time traveler from the sixties, which he really was.

"The mysteries of this world continue to confound me." He shoved his fists into his front pockets, a movement that made him look a lot like a twenty-first century guy.

Then he said, "If you can't control it, how are you going to get me back?"

Good question. I was saved from answering immediately by the appearance of Nate at the door. He wore a black graphic tee and dark jeans, and the way he dragged his hand through his hair made my heart skip a beat.

"You two coming in?" he said. "Breakfast is almost ready."

Nate's mom was a realtor, and she'd already left for her office by the time I got there. Nate's dad was a pilot, and was apparently somewhere over the Atlantic Ocean. So it was just the three of us.

Willie pointed to the bathroom. "I'll just make use of the latrine."

"He spent half the morning flushing the toilet and running the taps," Nate said. "You should've seen him when I explained the shower."

"Thanks for taking him in like this."

"It's fine. I like Willie, and after how he and his family have helped you, *us*, how could I not." Nate poured the last of the batter onto the electric grill. "The question is how are we going to get him back?" He steadied his eyes on me. "Unless you want to do this on your own?"

"No, I don't. I'm sorry for what happened at the Common. For what I did. It was a mistake."

Willie rejoined us before Nate could respond. I grabbed the syrup and milk jug from the fridge, as Nate flipped the final pancake on the grill and brought a plateful to the table.

"Electricity?" Willie said. "It makes that..." he pointed to the fridge.

"The refrigerator," I prompted

"The refrigerator cold, and the frying surface hot?"

"Yes."

"It provides energy for a lot of other things, too," Nate said, dishing out. "Afterwards I'll let you use my razor."

Willie's hand went to his chin, scrubbing the golden bristle growing there, and then he clasped both hands in front of him and bowed his head. I glanced at Nate. Willie was accustomed to praying before meals.

"Why don't you go ahead, Willie," Nate said.

"I'd be honored." He cleared his throat and said grace.

Willie was obviously starving and he wolfed down

several pancakes and a glass of milk before the comments started again. "This is delicious. I'm impressed Nathaniel, I'm not used to seeing a man cook a meal."

"Call me, Nate."

"My apologies. Nate."

Nate smiled politely, at Willie and then at me. A pit formed in my gut. I could tell that he'd only pushed down his anger at what I'd done. He hadn't truly forgiven me for it.

"In our time, domestic duties are shared between the sexes," I said, wanting to break through the tension between Nate and me. "Men can work at home if they want to and women can work outside the home."

"As equals? I suppose that explains the, uh," Willie's face flushed rosy with embarrassment, "unusual female attire."

I glanced down my sleeveless tank and Capris.

"You'll come to like it, my friend," Nate said with a smirk.

Willie chuckled. "I imagine it could grow on me. But on to more serious matters. How do I get back to my time? My family must be extremely worried."

Of course, his family had been dead for over a century, but I didn't point that out. Instead I explained what I knew, that he had to be touching me skin to skin when it happened. I didn't tell him how difficult it would be to get back, since I had almost no warning going from present to past. Unless we tried to trigger it again on purpose, like last time. Only, I didn't think public speaking would work twice; I just wouldn't be as nervous the second time around. We'd have to come up with something new. But what?

"Do they know I'm gone? Where do they think I went?"

I swallowed hard before answering. "Yes, they know you're gone."

Willie sat back and gasped. "They'll think I've deserted!"

I nodded slowly. "Probably." Unless Tim was able to come up with some kind of credible story. Which I doubted.

"That's a disgrace! And a crime!"

"I'm sorry." I said softly.

"Wait. It's been...oh, my." He suddenly looked stricken. "They're all dead now, aren't they?"

"In our time, yes," Nate said, "but not in yours."

"Right, good," Willie said, as if that brought him comfort. "I really need to get back before too much damage is done, then. Before my mother sets to grieving."

Nate cleared his throat. "I hate to eat and run. I have to work and I don't think my boss would appreciate if I didn't go into work again today."

I helped clean up, clearing the table as Nate loaded the dishwasher and wiped the counter.

"You do a lot of woman's work," Willie said from his seat at the table.

"It's not woman's work," I said. "It's just work."

Nate left us alone in the kitchen. We heard the bathroom tap running along with the swishing sound of Nate brushing his teeth.

Willie shook his head. "It's all just so incredible."

Nate knew how unlikely it was for me to trip two days in a row, which was why he was so nonchalant about leaving me. Either that, or he really didn't care if he went back with me again.

I actually wondered if he'd leave without kissing me goodbye, but he did come back for a quick kiss. Willie was there, so maybe that was why it was all I got.

Or maybe not.

My shoulders slumped as I watched him leave. Moments later the sound of his rusty '82 BMW's motor revving filtered through the screened front door. Then it disappeared as he drove away.

Willie drummed his fingers on the table. "You and Nathaniel aren't siblings."

Right. Totally forgot about that. Even in our tense state, it was pretty obvious that Nate and I didn't act like brother and sister. And we lived in different homes with different parents.

"No, we're not. It's kind of a long story." I went into the whole account about how Nate had asked me to dance on a dare, and how I'd accidentally taken him back.

"Like you accidentally brought me here," Willie mused.

"At the time we didn't even know each other except by reputation. I had no choice but to bring him with me to your farm and pass him off as my brother."

"I see."

"And," I rushed ahead, "we didn't become more than friends until much later."

"After Robert Willingsworth proposed?"

I stared at him. Of course he would remember that train wreck. "Yeah. After that."

The kitchen seemed awfully quiet while Willie studied me. I wondered what he was thinking. Was he completely freaked out? Did he just want to climb back into bed and hope this would all disappear?

Apparently not.

He stood and rubbed his hands together. "Well, since I'm here," he said. "Teach me about the future, Cassandra."

18

CASEY

THE BEST WAY to teach a teen the ins and outs of the twenty-first century? The mall.

I thought Boston on the first day would be a bit much, so I decided on the mall nearest to here. It wasn't exactly small potatoes. It had two floors, with a food court on the second. I had a flashback from a previous winter, my birthday, actually. Nate and I had just returned from a trip, and Jessica caught us together at the food court. She was so jealous she went public mean-girl on me.

And Nate broke up with her right there in front of everyone.

In his defense, she deserved it.

Willie and I walked to the bus stop near Nate's house. It had a route that went directly to the mall.

The bus was half-empty when we got on, and I let Willie have the window seat.

"I just can't believe all these buildings. There's almost no raw land left."

"There are still farms around here, but they're smaller," I said. "There are more if you get farther away from the city."

A black guy took the seat opposite us. He wore a blue sports jersey that stretched over a very large stomach; his head was shaved bald and he had white ear buds in his ears.

Willie leaned over to whisper. "What did that guy *eat*?"

I shrugged. "We have fast food now."

"*Fast* food?"

I thought of the food court. "Don't worry. I'll show you."

"What's he got in his ears?"

"Oh, he's listening to his iPod."

Willie raised his eyebrows. I dug through my purse and took out my phone. "We can store music in small devices like this. I tapped my music icon and a random song came through the small speakers.

Willie wrinkled his nose. "That's music?"

"Yup. Get Nate to show you MTV later."

"What's that?"

I could tell I'd be answering a lot of questions today. Wouldn't hurt to share some of the load with Nate. "Ask Nate later. He can give you the rundown on the TV."

Willie stopped with the questions for a while; I think he had a lot to process already.

The bus pulled into the mall parking lot. Willie whistled as we walked to the main entrance. "Wow."

I smiled. It was kind of fun to show off the future.

The mall was crowded with people–kids out of school, tourists, shoppers–on the lookout for summer specials.

Willie was taking it all in.

"It looks like we didn't have to worry about the Irish," he said.

"What do you mean?"

"In my time there is a social concern about immigration, especially the Irish and non-British Europeans."

I watched all the passing faces. African Americans, South Americans, and Asians mixed in with the white populace. "This is what Americans look like now."

When we got to the center of the mall, Willie stopped to stare up at the second story ceiling. A railing ran around the circumference of the upper level shops. People stopped to lean against them, and looked down at us.

"Incredible," Willie said. "Every doorway leads to another store?"

"Yeah. There are endless ways to spend your money."

We came upon an electronics shop that had dozens of flat screen TVs of every size flashing a western movie at a scene where everyone was shooting guns and falling to a dusty end.

Willie stared wide-eyed. "Is it real?"

"No, it's acting. Those aren't real bullets and that's not real blood."

"Acting?"

"Like a play, but they can film and broadcast it now."

We passed by *Forever21*, and I dragged Willie in to visit Lucinda.

"Hey there," she said when she saw us. Her brown eyes sparkled when they settled on Willie. "Wow, you look great."

Willie's face turned ten shades of red, "Oh, thanks. Nate lent me these."

"You totally fit in now, you know? You'd never guess you...weren't from here." She waved her hand. "So, what do you think?"

Willie still had that medicated, stunned look. "Uh, it's...interesting."

He watched one of the other customers flick through a rack of shirts along the wall and went over to do the same. Most of them had graphic images of icons like Bob Dylan, Jimi Hendrix and Marilyn Monroe on the fronts.

Lucinda leaned over and whispered, "He's adorable."

I pursed my lips. "He's not on the market."

"I know that. Geez, Casey. I can still admire the packaging, can't I? Even if it's a foreign product."

"Okay, fine. Then I agree." We watched as Willie checked out a rack of necklaces that had pewter pendants hanging from them, mostly skulls. His face twisted in alarm.

"He's cute," I said. "And charming. I see the appeal."

Other girls in the store had noticed, too. A couple huddled together close by, giggling.

Lucinda feigned anger and whispered under her breath. "Hey, stay away. He's mine."

My stomach growled.

"I'm taking Willie to the food court. Wanna come?"

"Can't. My break's not for another hour."

I caught Willie's eye and motioned for us to go. He said goodbye to Lucinda and she gave him a flirty wave. I shook my head at her and nudged Willie toward the escalator.

Willie tensed. "The steps are *moving*."

I took his arm. "It's okay. Perfectly safe."

Okay, it was kind of embarrassing the way he hung on to me for dear life, and it occurred to me he might be afraid of heights. How would a guy from around here in the nineteenth century even know he was afraid of heights? No tree or barn roof was ever this high off the ground.

"Almost there," I soothed. "Now look down, watch your step."

Willie stumbled onto the solid ground of the second

floor. He straightened out and smoothed his shirt, looking embarrassed. I grabbed his arm and pointed him in the direction of the food court.

"You wanted to learn about the future? Well, here's where you learn about the future of food." I waved an arm like Vanna White. "We have Japanese, Indian, Greek, Mexican, and American, aka, McDonalds."

I tried to describe what a Big Mac, fries and a milkshake were and finally gave up.

"The best way for you to understand is to taste it for yourself. Wait here."

I left Willie since I knew he didn't have any money, made an order for two McDonalds' classic meals, and paid with my debit card.

"You don't use paper bills to make purchases anymore?" Willie said when I returned.

"Oh, you can, but it's just easier this way."

"But they didn't keep your plastic card."

"No. There's a magnetic strip..." I stopped, realizing I wasn't even sure myself how it worked. "My card talks to my bank and the store's bank. When I make a purchase, the money goes directly from my account to theirs."

"I don't understand," Willie said. I pushed the burger in front of him

"Take a bite, and it won't matter."

I bit into mine at the same time as he did. Our orders were identical, but Willie made noises like he'd died and gone to heaven while eating his.

"Oh, my goodness." He nibbled a fry, sipped his chocolate milkshake and made more "yum" noises.

"I know. It's really a slow death poison, so I don't recommend eating it too often. But it just tastes so good."

"How much did your card have to pay for this?"

"About twelve dollars."

Willie almost dropped his burger.

"I know, cheap right? That's one of the reason's it's so popular."

"That's two weeks wages!"

Oh.

"Well, there's been a lot of inflation in the last hundred and fifty years. It's not that much now."

"Hey, Casey!"

I turned at my name and saw Kelly and Tyson. They'd gotten together around the same time Nate and I did. I waved them over. Tyson sauntered with his athletic strut, his dark fingers woven through Kelly's pale ones.

"Hey, guys," I said. I went to introduce Willie and paused. He was staring at their clasped hands, one black, one white.

"Willie," I said, making his gaze shift to my eyes. I'd have to explain the whole inter-racial-relationship-equality thing later. "These are my friends, Kelly and Tyson."

"This is Willie. Uh, a cousin." I didn't want it to look like I'd moved on from Nate. "He's just visiting."

"Pleased to meet you," Willie said.

Kelly sat beside me. "Terrible about Lucinda, huh?"

"What do you mean?" I said.

She tucked her blond hair behind one ear. "About Josh dumping her like that."

Willie narrowed his eyes.

I patted his hand and explained. "Lucinda and her boyfriend broke up."

"That's dreadful," Willie said. "Has her reputation been ruined?"

Tyson had taken the seat beside him and slapped him on the back. "You're funny, man."

Kelly shot Willie an annoyed look. "I feel so bad for her."

"He wasn't right for her," I said. "She'll find someone better."

"Like you did," Willie said, looking at me. "When you broke off your engagement with Robert Willingsworth."

My mouth dropped in horror.

"What?" Kelly said.

For some unfathomable reason, Willie felt like he needed to explain. "He was definitely wrong for her. He was wrong for any woman from the north."

Shut up, Willie. What was with the sudden bout of verbal diarrhea?

I faked a laugh. "Willie's such a kidder."

Tyson looked at me. "A cousin?"

"Distant cousin. Anyway, I think she's over Josh already. She's working today and Willie and I popped in to say hi. She seemed fine."

I offered Kelly my fries and Tyson the rest of my burger, since I'd suddenly lost my appetite. They accepted.

"Hey," Tyson said. "Did you hear about the shooting?"

I shook my head. "I've been too busy to follow the news."

"Some guy, only one block from my house, shot dead. They think it was a drug deal gone bad."

"Just acting," Willie said, his concerned look back in full force. "Right, Cassandra?"

"Cassandra?" Kelly said.

I glanced apologetically at Tyson and Kelly.

"No, this time it's real, Willie. We have a high crime rate here, compared... to where you're from."

"How's your brother?" Kelly asked. "I couldn't believe it when I heard he'd been shot at."

"Timothy was *shot* at?" Willie said. "Was he in battle?"

"He interrupted a bank robbery in progress." I gave Willie a stern look. *Stop asking me questions here.* Later, sure, but not in front of my friends.

"How is that cop that took the bullet?" Tyson asked, finishing up the milkshake I'd also pushed his way.

"Last I heard she was recovering well. Some major bruising, but nothing life threatening. Thank goodness she was wearing a vest." Tim and I and our parents had gone to visit her at the hospital. The media had gotten wind of it somehow and it made the back pages of the local paper.

Tyson stood, and Kelly followed suit. "Say hi to Nate for us," she said. "We'll have to go out together sometime. Nice to meet you, Willie."

Wow. That was exhausting. I was ready to dump Willie off at Nate's and go home, but I couldn't leave him alone there. We had to wait until Nate got off work.

Willie finished up the last of his meal, slurping the bottom of his milkshake with his straw.

"What'd you think?" I asked as he clung to me on our way down the escalator.

One side of his mouth lifted in a grin. "I think your future is a fascinating and frightening place."

19

TIM

I HAD BLISTERS the size of walnuts on the back of each ankle. Turns out thirty-five pounds is a lot heavier than you'd think, and walking in the humidity of summer, not the most pleasant experience. My clothes were drenched with sweat and I could've chugged back a gallon of water if they'd given it to me. I shook my near empty canteen and moaned.

That was the great thing about playing *War of the Universe.* You just got to sit there in the comfort of your own home, and the worst thing that happened was your thumbs or your butt grew numb. It was too bad the train couldn't take us all the way into Virginia, but there was talk of the Confederates sabotaging bridges. Sneaky Confederates.

Perfectly acceptable strategy in W of U.

Bummer for us soldiers.

We'd met up with other regiments along the way, and our numbers were getting totally impressive. In the thousands. I was surprised by how many of the guys looked like they should still be in school. I supposed I looked no different. It was hard to feed and water so many, so suddenly. I wasn't the only one to complain, especially on day two of our wilderness hike across the rolling hills in the northern tip of Virginia.

We followed General John Pope now. He had a flat face with thin hair that came to his earlobes and a full shaggy beard on his chin. The lucky dog got to ride a horse and was off scouting out our next campsite and plotting our next move.

We all collapsed to the ground when we reached the newly positioned Union flag. The wind blew at just the right speed, flapping it wide, a thirty-four star version that was apparently only a year old.

I lay my head on my knapsack and stared at the clouds rolling across the sky. Instead of the teddy bears and bunnies my mind used to see when I was a kid, the clouds took the shape of steam engine trains and musket rifles. Mine rested against my chest, and I stroked the barrel with my hand. I still couldn't believe I was here experiencing this. Despite my aching limbs, I was excited.

"Are you smiling?" Joseph said. "You must share your secret to the blissful life."

"I have no secret, young grasshopper," I said. "Except to grasp each day as a new adventure."

"Forgive me for saying so," he countered, "but you say the oddest things."

"As do you."

I breathed deeply of the alfalfa, happy I didn't have an allergy to that particular plant. The breeze dried the sweat off my face.

A bugle blew and that was our sign to get to work.

"I thought that was your job," I said to Joseph.

He shifted his shoulders back in an attempt to look taller. "I'm not the only bugle player."

A low groan traveled amongst the troops as the men pulled themselves off the ground and began to set up camp.

Joseph was my tent mate. We each carried half a white tent canvas that buttoned together at the top. We set them up in rows, thousands of small, pointy white tents like sharks teeth.

Joseph sat around the fire we'd built and polished his bugle. "This is my weapon."

"It's a beauty," I said, relieved that this frail boy wasn't going to be thrust into the front of the line.

"Different musical combinations mean different military actions," Joseph explained. "Men in the midst of battle can't hear the shouts of the commander near the back. The bugle cry tells them when to press on and when to retreat."

Of course I'd already been instructed in the different bugle commands, but I allowed the boy to feel like the authority in his field.

Henry and James shared the tent beside us and joined us around the fire as dusk fell. The worst part of this whole thing so far was the food. Exceptionally disgusting. The ration varied. A bit of dried beef. Sometimes beans, and this revolting patty that was supposed to be the vegetable portion of our meal. It was supplemented with a few rock hard crackers. I waved mine in front of the guys.

"Seriously?" I said. "This is what they fed you?"

Henry shot me a strange look, and I realized I'd slipped into past tense. "I mean, this is what they feed us?"

"Sheet-iron crackers," James quipped. "Taste like wood, but they last forever."

"Let's try boiling them," Henry said, pouring water from

his canteen into his tin dipper. It did make them softer, but no tastier. When Joseph cooked up the coffee substitute, something truly horrendous made from charred green peas, I almost deserted, there and then. Gross.

James feigned a gag. "If not death by musket, then death by army rations. We're doomed either way, men."

Down the row we could hear one of the men playing one of those kazoo things I'd found in my haversack.

"Guy's got talent," I said. "You better watch out, Joseph. You could lose your job in the military band."

The flames grew brighter as the night grew darker. Yawns echoed around the camp and one by one the orange spots that dotted the field went dark, until all the men slipped into their little white tents.

Henry was the first around our fire to bid us good night. We heard his low murmur through the thin canvas. *"Though I walk through the valley of the shadow of death, I will fear no evil..."*

20

CASEY

THE NEXT DAY was Saturday, which meant Nate had the day off and could help with Willie duty.

"He was pretty freaked out last night," Nate said when he called me. "What were you thinking?"

"What do you mean? He wanted me to teach him about the future."

"So you took him to *the mall*? Haven't you heard of baby steps?"

"You didn't give me a *to-do* list before you left." I sighed. We sounded like an old married couple. "What're you going to do with him today?"

"I'll introduce him to the world of television and electronic games. Should keep him amused for the rest of the day and out of trouble."

I wished I could join them. The mood around my house was dark, and I had the feeling Mom and Dad were preparing for the worst.

"We need to get him back," I said, very aware of the pronoun "we."

"I know," he said.

I swallowed and pressed on. "Dad's home this morning, but he has to work later. He wants me to stay home, so my mom won't be left alone again."

"Don't worry, we'll be fine."

I spent the morning cleaning the kitchen and vacuuming and dusting the rest of the house. Mom had let the place go since Tim's disappearance. Dad was in his home office talking to someone from the local news station. They wanted to make a public appeal.

In the afternoon I tended to the pile of papers on Mom's desk, scanning what needed to be scanned, entering numbers in her accounting program, filing everything else.

I was getting antsy about staying away from Willie for too long. I never knew when the next trip would hit, and I had to be touching him when it did if I was going to get him home.

I peeked into Dad's office. He was slumped over his computer, his broad shoulders folding in and making him seem smaller than usual. I'd grown used to him being gone when he'd left, and it took awhile to get used to him being around all the time again when he moved back in.

"How's it going?" I said.

He sighed and ran a hand over his head. "Well, I'm organizing a poster blitz. I've put an ad in the paper, and they're running a story on the six o'clock news. Someone out there knows something."

I nodded and swallowed hard.

"You'll ask your friends to help with the blitz?"

"Of course."

.   .   .

WHEN I LEFT the house the next morning to catch the bus to Nate's, I was surprised to hear the lawn mower going in the front yard. That was Tim's job and I knew Dad had already left for work.

My heart jumped a bit when I saw who it was.

"Chase?"

I waved my arms so he'd notice me over the noise.

He grinned and turned the mower off.

"Hey, Casey."

"What are you doing?"

He glanced at the mower and then back to me. "I think they call this mowing the lawn."

"Yeah, but why? Did my dad hire you?"

"No. I was mowing our lawn, and I could see that yours needed it, too. I know your brother's...not around, and this was probably his job, right?"

I nodded and a lump formed in my throat. All the stress with Tim and Willie. And Nate. There was something about this random act of kindness that moved me. A tear escaped and ran down my face.

"That's very nice of you."

He reached over and gently wiped the tear from my cheek. "I'm happy to do it."

The electricity that zipped through my body at his touch shocked me and I stepped back.

"Oh. Um, I have to go."

He held my gaze, which rattled me further. "I'll see you later," he said.

I walked away, then I turned back, knowing he would be watching me.

"My dad has a poster blitz planned for later today. Do you want to come?"

His eyes sparkled. "You bet I do."

I TAPPED on Nate's front door out of courtesy and walked in without invitation. Nate and Willie were intensely competing in a racing game on Nate's massive flat screen TV.

I watched from behind the couch. Willie was losing, but not doing so bad for a guy who'd never seen an automobile before three days ago.

He smiled up at me. "The future is fun. Do you want to play?"

Nate offered me his controls. "Here, use mine. I feel bad beating the guy over and over again."

"And you don't think I could beat him?"

"That's not what I meant."

The controls were still warm from Nate's grip. He left the room but returned with three cans of soda. He pulled the tabs and offered them to us.

"Another modern beverage?" Willie asked.

"It's carbonated." I took a sip. "You'll like it."

Willie's face pinched together as he swallowed, then he let out a belch.

Nate and I laughed. Willie grew red with embarrassment. "My apologies."

"It's an occupational hazard," Nate said

"And this?" Willie asked, tapping the can. "It's too light to be tin."

"Aluminum."

Our attention was drawn to a knock on the door. Lucinda stuck her head in, "Hello?"

"Hey, Luce," I said, waving her in.

She'd texted me when I was on the bus and I told her I was headed here.

Lucinda wore a short, flouncy skirt and a pair of cute sandals. Her long, straight dark hair hung like a glossy sheet down her back and she had a little too much make-up on what was already a flawless face.

Something told me she hadn't gone to the trouble of looking that good for me and Nate. Her smile brightened as she locked eyes with Willie.

His face lit up, too, and he was apparently equally happy to see her. She wiggled her fingers.

I needed to get Lucinda and Tim together in a room and preach to them about the follies of cross-century relationships.

"I thought Willie might like to see the sights," she said.

"He's seen the mall." I was surprised at how irritated I felt.

"Oh, wow. *The mall.*" She turned to Willie. "But you want to see more than the mall, right? Don't you want to see more of the future?"

Willie stood and spoke without taking his eyes off of her. "Yes, indeed. I am here, and I might as well take every opportunity to experience it."

Lucinda was quick to volunteer. "I'd be happy to take you sightseeing."

"I don't know. What if..." I started.

Lucinda looped her arm in Willie's. "You can come if you want to."

"Could I have a word, Lucinda?" I motioned with my head to the kitchen. She reluctantly let go of Willie's arm and followed me.

"What?"

"Oh, I was just wondering how you were, with you know, your heartbreak over Josh."

"Josh who?"

"Very funny."

"You were right, Josh wasn't the one."

"And you think Willie *is?*

"Come on, Case, I'm not dating Willie. I just want to hang out. Get my mind off Josh. And I think Willie could use the distraction, too."

"Believe me, he's got plenty of distractions. I just don't want you rebounding off of him. He's not going to be here for very long."

"I know that. Which is exactly why he's the perfect guy to hang out with. You worry too much, Casey. We'll be fine." She dragged me back to the living room before I could say anything more.

Nate had turned the games off and a news channel had taken its place. Images of starving kids in Somalia, bloody clashes in Syria, gang deaths in New York filled the living room one after the other.

Willie blanched. "Acting?"

I shook my head. "I'm afraid not."

Nate shut it off. "Where are you planning to go?" he said to Lucinda. "Maybe we can meet up with you later?"

Lucinda started twisting her hair with her finger, a sure sign that she was into Willie more than she admitted. "Oh, I'd thought I'd start with Harvard, let Willie have a better look this time. Then, maybe a museum, possibly go into Boston."

I didn't want her going as far away as Boston, who knew what kind of trouble they could get in there.

"You know," I said, remembering how nervous I was about letting Willie out of my sight, "we should go with you."

I glanced at Nate with a look that said, "Help?"

He grabbed his keys. "We can take my car."

I couldn't help but read more into that. Maybe I was being paranoid, but we hadn't been alone together since the "incident" at the Commons. And now he didn't want to be in the back seat of Lucinda's car alone with me.

Nate drove north on Broadway.

"How fast is this contraption going?" Willie said. I looked back to see him white knuckling the door grip.

"Only thirty-five miles an hour," Nate answered "Traffic's crawling today."

"Thirty-five miles an hour!" Willie whistled.

Willie had his head out the window like a red-haired dog, taking in all the sights.

Nate pulled into a parking lot at Harvard Square.

"This is Harvard University," I said. "Some of it. It's quite vast now."

Willie stared, his mouth gaping. "So many more buildings... and people than in my day."

I nodded. I'd been to Harvard College 1862 only a couple days earlier.

"We could go to the Museum of Natural History," Lucinda said. "Or the art museum."

Willie looked at her like she was the only girl in the whole place. "Why don't you choose?"

She giggled and said, "Okay. I'm in the mood for art."

Nate and I walked behind Lucinda and Willie and I watched wistfully as they joked around and laughed. Lucinda touched Willie's arm repeatedly, and by the time we got to the end of the Common, they were holding hands.

I sneaked a look at Nate and saw that he was watching them, too.

Then he turned to me, and took my hand, pulling me close. "I'm sorry I've been such a tool lately."

"I'm sorry, too."

He kissed me on the forehead, and I sighed with relief. We were going to be okay.

The university grounds were massive. Actually, there were facilities connected to Harvard in Boston and other areas you couldn't walk to from here, so it wasn't too surprising that we'd gotten a little lost.

Before we reached the art museum, we happened upon Memorial Hall, an elaborate brick building with impressive stone arches and a high medieval-like tower. The windows were intricate pieces of stained glass. It looked more like a church than a theatre.

We stopped to read the plaque.

"Proposed by a group of Harvard graduates after the Civil War, the Memorial Hall was built as a memorial to Harvard graduates who bravely fought for the Union, and as a gathering space and theater for college alumni. Featuring a grand tower that was completed in 1877, stained glass windows, marble tablets and the Sanders Theatre, the building is owned by Harvard University."

WE TOOK a tour inside and were appropriately awed by the masterful craftsmanship found inside and also sobered by the fact that it was inspired by the death of Harvard students in the Civil War. The same war that Willie had fought in, and that Tim was still engaged with.

"How long did it go on?" Willie asked.

This was one question I'd hoped to avoid, but he deserved the truth.

"Four years."

Willie's Adam's apple bobbed as he swallowed hard, like he'd expected bad news and got it.

We almost stopped breathing when we came across this: A Hymn by Oliver Wendell Holmes for the ceremony held on October 6, 1870, to lay the Memorial Hall cornerstone.

> *"Not with the anguish of hearts that are breaking*
> *Come we as mourners to weep for our dead;*
> *Grief in our breasts has grown weary with aching,*
> *Green is the turf where our tears we have shed.*
> *While o'er their marbles the mosses are creeping*
> *Stealing each name and its record away.*
> *Give their proud story to memory's keeping,*
> *Shrined in the temple we hallow today.*
> *Hushed are their battlefields, ended their marches.*
> *Deaf are their ears to the drumbeat of mourn-*
> *Rise from the sod ye far columns and arches!*
> *Tell their bright deeds to the ages unborn.*
> *Emblem and legend may fade from the portal,*
> *Keystone may crumble and portal may fall;*
> *They were the builders whose work is immortal,*
> *Crowned with the dome that is over us all."*

LUCINDA PLUCKED a tissue from her bag and wiped carefully under her mascara-laden eyes. "It's so sad," she whispered hanging onto Willie's hand.

Nate and I followed them outside.

"So, what should we do next?" Nate said.

Willie answered. "Is there a library nearby?"

"You want to go to the library?" Lucinda asked, surprised.

"There would be a record of the war, wouldn't there? Of my family?"

And the question he left unasked: a record of him, the deserter.

"I don't know if that's a good idea," I said. I already questioned the wisdom of this tour of the future.

"Please," Willie pleaded. "I need to know."

"The Cambridge Public Library is on site." I sighed and pointed in the general direction. "We can walk from here."

Like many landmarks in Cambridge and Boston, the library was a mix of old and new. The old part was built in 1888 and made of stone with large front arches over the entrance and a turret that made it look like a church or a small castle. Attached was a much larger two story rectangular glass and steel structure only a few years old.

"Willie?" I said, touching his shoulder as we headed for the entrance. He looked a little downcast. "How are you holding up?"

He shrugged limply. "None of this was here. Even the 'historical' part of this library wasn't around. It's fascinating but sad for me at the same time."

"We don't have to do this if you don't want to," I said. "I mean, we can come back tomorrow."

His head shot up. "I'll still be here tomorrow, won't I? How long *will* I be here?"

My eyes darted sideways toward Nate and he jumped in. "These things take time. We just have to be patient."

Willie sucked in like he was bracing himself. "I'm ready."

It was almost as bright inside as out, with all the glass windows. I led the way to the research counter and spoke quietly to the research librarian telling her we wanted to learn about local soldiers in the Civil War. My request didn't faze her and she took us to shelves that housed books on genealogy and local history.

"You'll also find information on the library website." She pointed out the row of computers available for public use.

Willie had a perplexed expression and I wondered if Nate had explained the internet to him yet.

Nate immediately left the book area and headed for a computer terminal. I couldn't help but watch poor Willie's face as Nate typed and the screen came to life.

"A TV?" he said.

"A computer. Information traveling on..." I stopped. I feared Willie was suffering from information overload. I pulled out a chair for him. "Here, have a seat."

A page on the library website called Massachusetts Civil War Research Center opened up. Nate read aloud.

"This site contains a comprehensive collection of information pertaining to soldiers, sailors, and marines who served in Massachusetts units and regiments during the Civil War. Information found on this site was taken in part from documents prepared, compiled, and published by the Adjutant General's Office of Massachusetts in 1888."

Nate used the scroll down feature and the list of all the infantries appeared.

"What infantry were you in, Willie?"

His answer came out in a whisper. "The thirteenth."

Nate clicked on the Thirteenth Massachusetts. Then he

typed in Watson. "There you are." Nate pointed to the screen. "William D. Watson."

We all stared at the screen, and my blood grew cold right down to my toes. Everyone stiffened as they read the text in front of us.

It mentioned the battle of Chancellorsville, May 4, 1863.

"I die?" Willie whispered.

21

TIM

HURRY UP and wait.

Too many bugs, too much heat and hunger. Way too much time. I wished now I'd paid attention to the Civil War unit in my history class. I was as clueless as the rest of the guys here as to when the next fight for this regiment would happen.

I moved into the tent to escape the heat and moments later I'd inch back outside for a breath of fresh air. A vicious mind-sucking cycle. When my stomach growled, I dug through my rations. I pulled out the dried, desiccated veggie thing. It looked like a piece of cow dung.

I waved it around like a prize. "How d'ya eat this?"

Henry presented his tin dipper. "I made a soup."

Okay. I put the mini cow pie in my tin dipper and added water. I held it over the fire in the same manner as Henry.

"Heard from Sara?" I asked.

Letter writing and receiving was a big event. On slow days like this, the scratching of pencils was almost louder than the birds. Of course, I never wrote anyone or got any letters. When the guys asked me about it, I just shrugged and said most of my family didn't know how to write.

"Yes, she's fine, though terribly worried about her brother, as we all are."

I studied this stocky, quiet, serious guy.

"You plan on marrying her?"

Henry seemed startled by my direct question, but he answered it anyway.

"Yes." He got all dreamy-eyed. "Sara is an amazing woman. Strong, intelligent, beautiful."

Wow. He was smitten.

He looked up from the fire and asked, "Is there a special girl at home for you?"

"Nah." I said and stirred my vegetable/cow dung soup.

I prided myself for not getting serious like some of my friends had. They just got burned in the end. I liked my "relationships" short and sweet.

"What'd you do, you know, before the war?" I asked him.

"My father is in banking. I'm following his footsteps." Henry turned the question back. "How about you?"

"Oh, just school," I said.

I couldn't exactly tell him I delivered pizza, not that he would even know what that meant. Although now he probably wondered why no one could write if we went to school, but before he could ask more probing questions, I turned the topic back to my so-called soup.

"Is that chunk cabbage or cauliflower?" I asked.

James and Joseph joined us then. "They're handing out coffee and sugar."

Henry jumped up along with half the regiment, but I stayed put. I was a coffee snob, Americano with cream. I couldn't stomach what they passed off for coffee here.

I sipped my soup while James and Joseph cooked their coffee. Joseph didn't look old enough to drink it, but he didn't look old enough to be a soldier in the army, either. Not even as just a bugle player. He looked equally out of place in the evenings when the guys puffed on their pipes.

I was curious about James and his friendship with Willie. Willie was going to need someone solid when he got back, and I wondered how he was coping with being in the future.

"So, James, what's up with Willie, do you think?" I said.

He cast me a dark look, the kind that made me glad I was on his side in this war.

"What do you mean?"

"Well, you're friends, right?"

"We are. Have been since we were youngsters. We attend the same church. We attended the same school house." His lips pulled up into a slight smile. "We liked to cause a little trouble for Mrs. Wyatt, our teacher. Willie and I would sit on opposite sides of the room and make cricket noises. Mrs. Wyatt would scour the room looking for the insect. When she figured out it was a couple of us kids, she tried to catch who was doing it, but she never did."

He sipped his coffee and gazed out at the meadow. "I don't understand what happened to him. He wouldn't just leave without telling me about it."

"I think he'll show up again with a good explanation," I said.

James settled his blue eyes on my face. "I hope you're right."

Henry came back with his coffee ration. "Prepare to pack up," he said. "I overheard some talk. The General is about to call us back to marching. Seems a battle is awaiting."

Yes. I jumped to my feet to start packing. *It was about time.*

22

CASEY

LUCINDA GRABBED Willie's arm. "You don't have to go back." Then she pierced me with her deep brown eyes. "He doesn't have to go back, right?"

Truth was, I didn't know. How was I to know if Willie's sudden disappearance from his natural time line didn't upset the universe in some way, like that whole Butterfly Effect thing? This was one huge butterfly.

On the other hand, making Willie go back now felt like a death sentence.

"If you don't go back," I said quietly, as the librarian was starting to give us the evil eye, "you'll never see your family again."

"But if he dies, they wouldn't see him again anyway," Lucinda persisted. She obviously had stronger feelings for Willie than she'd admitted to. The girl definitely had a thing for redheads.

"She has a point there," Nate added. Now I felt like the bad guy. It wasn't like I wanted to see Willie dead.

Willie lowered his head. "This might sound really selfish, but I don't want to die."

I reached for his hand. "That's not selfish, it's normal. You don't have to make your mind up right now."

"Casey," Lucinda said sharply. "Don't touch him."

I scowled at her. Was she making the decision for him?

"I wish there was someone we could talk to about this," Nate said. "We have to be sure that whatever we decide doesn't have repercussions."

"Like Willie staying is going to start the third world war?" Lucinda snapped, clearly annoyed. "It would be wrong for us to insist he go back."

"Wait a minute," I said, an idea forming. "I know who we could talk to."

"Who?" They said this practically in unison. Now we did get the librarian's evil eye.

I lowered my voice and leaned in. "Samuel."

"Our Samuel?" Willie said. "He's still alive?"

"Yes, but he's changed a lot since you've seen him last."

Nate and I started visiting Samuel regularly after his sister Rosa died. By a strange twist of fate, we'd discovered Rosa was my dad's biological mother, which made her my grandmother and Samuel my uncle.

"Samuel was born in 1944, which makes him sixty-eight today," I said.

Willie shook his head. "I just saw him a few months ago. He was a teenager."

"He was looping from the sixties when I accidentally accompanied him on his loop." I explained how I ended up going to 1961 with Samuel when I was on my own loop to Willie's time.

"It's so confusing," he said. "But, if there are two time-travelers, could there be more?"

"I only know of one more, a girl I met last year in a convenience store. I saw the raccoon eyes form on her face and her demeanor change from cheerful to confused in a second. Her name was Adeline."

"Did she share your loop?" Willie asked. Nate and Lucinda had already heard this story, but Willie was all ears.

"No, she said she looped to the nineteen fifties. I haven't been able to track her down since. I wish I would've gotten her number. She mentioned something about moving west with her dad."

"Maybe you could put an ad out," Lucinda said. "Looking for blond teen time-traveler who recently moved from Cambridge to Hollywood."

I grunted. "Like that wouldn't attract the wackos."

Nate pulled into a row of single story, fifty-five plus, brick townhouses, stopping in front of number twenty-four.

"Maybe we should've called first," I said.

"Nah, he'll be thrilled to see us," said Nate. "Especially Willie."

I actually wasn't so sure about that. And he might not be too impressed with my carelessness in bringing someone from the past to the future. We *had* warning coming back, and he knew that.

I knocked tentatively on the door. "Maybe he's napping," I said, but then the door cracked open.

"Hi, Samuel!" My voice sounded un-naturally cheerful. "We have a surprise."

As I suspected, his bright toothy grin disappeared when his eyes settled on Willie. "Oh, my. You best come in," he said.

He turned and shuffled into the sitting room. We scuttled in behind him, and stood awkwardly.

Lucinda spoke first. "Hi, Mr. Jones."

Then Nate added, "It's nice to see you again."

Willie offered a timid, "Hello."

"Hello to you, Master Willie," Samuel replied.

I jumped in. "You don't have to call him master, Uncle Sam."

"And you don't have to call me uncle."

It was a slip. My dad insisted I call him that, so I had to when Dad was around.

Samuel ran a hand through his gray curls. "I feel like such an old man." He pushed his glasses up on his nose. Though his skin creased around his eyes, his cheeks remained full and soft like dark, tanned leather.

"Take a seat," he said, with a voice that had aged like old tree bark. "I'll get tea."

I offered to help. Samuel's kitchen was small with a U shaped counter top. The walls were off-white with a window above the sink. The fridge was apartment-sized but large enough for the minimal grocery items Samuel kept in there. I opened it to get the milk.

"It was an accident," I whispered as I took five teacups and saucers out of the cupboards. "It's no big deal, right?"

"That depends." The whistle blew and Samuel filled the teapot. "What's he missing by not being there?"

"Death?"

Samuel raised a bushy gray eyebrow.

"And what else?"

"I don't know. Is there anything else?"

I carried the tray into the sitting room, placing it on the

coffee table in front of the others who had crammed onto the room's only sofa.

"Sugar?" I asked.

I pointed to the box of sugar but left everyone to make up their own drink.

Willie took a moment to examine his portion of sugar, neatly hardened and packed into a cube, before dropping it into his tea. "We think of everything in the future, don't we?" he said.

Samuel sat in the lone recliner and a gray, tabby cat jumped onto his lap. "Hey, Watson," he said, petting it.

"You named your cat, Watson?" Willie asked.

Samuel grinned. "The name brings back memories. Mostly good."

We all took long quiet sips of our tea.

Samuel placed his cup in its saucer with a shaky hand. "Casey filled me in a little in the kitchen."

Lucinda cleared her throat. "Did she tell you that Willie will die in the Civil War if he goes back? He doesn't have to go back, does he?"

"I certainly wouldn't want to put Willie in harm's way intentionally."

"Good," Lucinda said grabbing Willie's arm. "That settles it, Willie stays."

When did she become the boss of us?

"Samuel?" I said.

Samuel pushed the cat off his lap, and pulled a piece of string out of the side pocket of his recliner.

"Watson loves to play with it," he said in way of explanation. He laid it out in a flat line on the coffee table.

"Imagine this string goes in either direction for infinity. This is time."

Then he took his finger and made loops with the tips touching each other. "This is still infinite time. But every once in a while, in ways I don't understand, time folds for a specific individual, and two time zones, if you will, touch each other."

I hadn't thought of it like that before, but it made sense. Sort of.

"Say this is you, Casey," Samuel took a pen and made a mark at the top of one loop, "and this is Willie." He made another dot on the top of the neighboring loop. The dots were close enough to each other that they touched.

He pulled the string flat. "It's still you, in the same place, but in your own time." He looped the string again, until the two dots touched. "It's you, Casey, in folded time. It feels like you've gone to the past, but you've actually only been folded up next to it. Make sense?"

I looked at the others and we all had a blank look. "I guess."

"Even though your time is folding, your life *unfolds* as it should. But," he looked up to make sure we got the next thing he had to say. "Willie here has jumped loops."

Samuel flattened the string and crossed out the first dot. Then he added a new one next to mine. "His life hasn't unfolded naturally. Everything that will happen and has happened between here and here," he pointed to Willie's two dots, "has been changed."

"So, it's changed." Lucinda said. "Does it matter?"

Samuel leaned back in his recliner. "That's up to you to find out."

23

CASEY

WE STOPPED at a fast food Mexican place to regroup, though I found my appetite lacking in a big way.

Mexican blankets, cha-chas and other themed trinkets decorated the bright yellow walls. Spanish string music pumped through a bad sound system. The place smelled of taco spice, cilantro and cheese.

"They bring food all the way up from Mexico?" Willie said, staring wide-eyed at the bright menu board that hung behind the counter above our heads.

"Oh, you're so cute." Lucinda nudged up beside him. "You've really never eaten a taco before?"

We got our orders and took a seat by the window overlooking the highway. Willie and Lucinda sat across from Nate and me in a booth with royal-blue fiberglass benches. Lucinda had her flirt on high and touched Willie's arm every two seconds, totally oblivious to the embarrassment on Willie's face. He wouldn't be used to girls being so forward. I felt like kicking Lucinda under the table, but she sat kitty-corner from me and I was afraid I'd nick Willie instead.

Nate knocked his leg against mine as he bit into his burrito, and I knocked him back. It was like we were trying to speak without speaking. We were still there for each other, even if we screwed up once in a while. There was so much I wanted to say to him, but it had to wait until we were alone. And probably until we had this difficult situation sorted out.

"What should we do?" I said softly, not that I had to worry about Lucinda and Willie hearing us. She had him captivated with stories about high school life in the twenty-first century and how much Willie was going to enjoy Cambridge High.

The next thing you knew, she'd be proposing.

"We need to find out more about Willie," Nate said. "The 1862 Willie. And about his family, what happened to them in the last 150 years."

"The Turner house is a museum now," I said.

Nate smiled. "Good idea. Let's go there."

WE ALL AGREED TO GO, but first we had to do the poster blitz for my parents.

A crowd was gathered on our driveway and front lawn, friends of my parents, neighbors we'd known forever, Tim's friends, my friends. My dad handed out printed copies of Tim's picture with a phone number and a promise of a reward on them. My heart sank. I felt so bad that we were wasting these people's time like this and getting my parents' hopes up. They both had dark circles under their eyes and looked like they'd aged ten years.

I'm so sorry.

I searched the group for signs of Chase, but couldn't see him anywhere. I was surprised by the measure of disappointment I felt. I shook it off. Across the yard I saw Officer Clarice Porter. She was in plain clothes and at first I didn't recognize her. Her husband Wade was also on the force. He was tall, built like a footballer, and he towered over his much smaller wife. I went to them to say hello.

"Hi, Casey," Clarice said. Her hair was out of her standard bun, falling in dark waves down her back, and you could tell she was in shape by the way her jeans fit. The Porters were a good-looking couple.

"It's so nice of you to come out today," I said. "My parents and I really appreciate your support."

"No problem. I'm still on medical leave until the end of the month, but I feel fine. Anything we can do to help, we'll do. You know that, right?"

I almost teared up at her kindness.

"Thanks, that means a lot."

"Our best people are on this case. They'll find your brother."

Oh, I wished she hadn't added that last part. I felt so bad that all these people were worrying and working, and it was my fault.

I said goodbye and headed back toward Nate and the gang when I felt hands grab my shoulders from behind.

"Casey! I made it."

I spun around and Chase almost ran me over. As it was, he stood very, very, close. I could smell his aftershave, and see the small crinkles around his eyes when he smiled.

"Hey." I took a small tiny step backward. "I'm glad you could make it."

He rocked back on his sneakers. "I wouldn't miss it."

Then he followed me to my group, and I introduced him to Lucinda, Willie and Nate. Chase scowled a little at Nate, and I remembered that he thought Nate had hit me. Nate barely lifted his chin to acknowledge Chase.

We picked up our posters from the pile on the table Dad had set up outside, and marked off the area we'd be blitzing on the map he'd laid out.

Tim's friends came in behind us, led by Alex. I felt bad for him, knowing it must be hard for him, too, to have his best friend go "poof".

I turned to offer some words of comfort, but he'd fallen back, and was talking earnestly to someone. When he twisted slightly, I saw that it was Chase. How did they know each other already?

Chase saw me watching and sprinted over. "I don't think we'll all fit into your boyfriend's car." He gestured to his Mustang in the driveway next door. "Do you want to come with me?"

"Oh, I don't know." Nate and Willie and Lucinda were opening the doors to Nate's BMW. It wouldn't be fair to make Chase drive alone, and I was the only one he actually knew, even a little bit. "Wait, just a moment."

I skipped over to Nate's car. "Hey, guys. I should probably go with Chase. He's new, and doesn't know how to get there..."

There was a moment of really awkward silence. Nate's face sealed up like a stone. Lucinda looked a little stunned by my choice, too. Willie was the only one who didn't seem to register the tension.

He turned to Lucinda. "In that case, would you prefer the front seat?"

"Uh, no, you go ahead." Then she mouthed to me, *What are you doing?*

I shrugged. I wasn't sure. I felt caught.

My hand started sweating on the posters, and I shifted them to my other arm. When I turned to go with Chase, he had a bemused smirk on his face.

"That went well," he said.

"What do you mean?"

"I was being sarcastic. Your friends don't like me."

"They like you. They're just..."

He opened the passenger door for me when we reached his car. "They're just worried I'll steal you from your boyfriend."

I gasped at his forwardness and felt my face grow rosy.

He laughed as he got in and put his seatbelt on. "Don't worry. I won't put any moves on you." He shot me a super-sexy grin. "Today."

24

CASEY

CHASE LIED. The whole time we were out putting up posters, he had *his flirt* on. He'd touch my shoulders or my back as he passed by, and "accidentally" rub up against me. He'd aim sly grins and pouty lips in my direction. He and Lucinda should enter a flirt competition. Except Lucinda wasn't blatantly flirting in front of Willie's girlfriend.

By the time we'd pinned up all the posters, Nate was fuming. "I'm going to punch that guy in the face pretty soon," he muttered in my ear.

When it was time to go home, Nate pointed to the front seat of his car, and said to me, "Get in."

"Hey, I can take her home," Chase said, faking inno-cence. "It's kind of on my way."

It actually made sense to me. No point in Nate driving all the way to my house first when Chase lived right next door.

"It's getting late," I said. "I'll meet up with you guys again tomorrow."

Nate grabbed my arm and pulled me close. Then he laid one on me, good and hard, straight on the lips. I could tell it wasn't for my benefit. He was staking his territory in front of Chase. Like a dog peeing on a fire hydrant.

I pushed him away, furious. "What was that?"

I didn't wait for an answer. I fumed as I stormed to Chase's car. I fastened my seatbelt and folded my arms tightly across my chest.

Chase didn't seem to be in the same kind of rush. He meandered slowly over, opening the driver's door, and sliding in, just as Nate squealed away.

"Trouble in paradise?" His eyes sparkled with amusement.

I huffed. "No thanks to you."

"Why?"

"You know why." What a couple of juveniles. "Just take me home."

I didn't bother to thank Chase or to say goodnight when we got there.

THE NEXT MORNING I heard a light rap on the front door and when I looked out, there was a bouquet of flowers on the front step. They were hand clipped, tied together with string, and placed in a jar filled with water. I assumed they were for my parents, but when I checked the card, it had my name on it.

Casey, I'm sorry. I crossed the line last night. I can't help that I like you. Forgive me?

I turned towards the Miller yard, and there stood Chase with his hands clasped in front of him and his chin lowered all repentant-like. I had to admit, he was very cute.

I found myself walking toward him. "You didn't have to do this."

"I know, but I really am sorry. I overstepped last night, and put you in an uncomfortable position."

"Yeah, you made my boyfriend's black list."

He bristled a bit at the use of the word *boyfriend*. "Well, I don't really care about his blacklist. I just want to make sure I'm not on yours."

"You're not." I grinned. "Thanks for coming to help."

"Anytime."

I stood there with Chase's flowers in my hand feeling awkward. And kind of special. It was such a sweet gesture and I hadn't gotten flowers from anyone before. Not even from Nate.

"Well, I should go," I said taking a step away.

"Casey?"

"Yes?"

"Will you go out with me sometime?"

Wow, I hadn't expected that. This guy knows how to go after what he wants.

"I *have* a boyfriend."

He shrugged, grinning crookedly. "I know. You've made that pretty clear. But he's not your husband."

I had to laugh. "So that's where you'd draw the line? If I were married?"

"Maybe."

This guy was living up to his name. "I can't, but thanks for asking."

The grin never left his face. "Another time, then."

I felt myself blush, leaving Chase to stare after me. Again.

Nate was coming for me that morning. He texted that he felt bad about me taking the bus all the time lately. It was nice he finally noticed, but I was pretty sure he was more concerned Chase might offer to drive me.

Now that Chase had made it clear he was looking for more than friendship, things really could get awkward.

I put the flowers on the table and poured myself a cup of coffee. Mom hadn't gotten out of bed yet, but Dad was in his office, so I peeked in.

"Hey, sunshine," he said. "How are you?"

"I'm fine."

He leaned back in his leather office chair, and took off his reading glasses. "Are you sure? I know we've been busy with... dealing with..."

"It's okay, Dad. I understand. Believe me."

"I just don't want you feeling like we've forgotten that you're still here."

I put my coffee down to give him a hug. "I haven't."

I heard a knock and someone coming through the front door. Nate's voice floated down the hall. "Casey?"

"I gotta go, Dad. I'll be home later."

I found Nate in the kitchen, reading the card he found tucked in the flowers.

"This guy's after you," he stated through tight lips.

I shrugged and then denied it. I couldn't see how it would help for Nate to know Chase had asked me out.

Nate's eyes held mine. "He understands our relationship, right?"

"Yes."

"To be clear, he knows I'm your boyfriend?"

Didn't I just answer that? *"Yes."*

"I don't like that guy."

No kidding. "He was being a little forward last night, but he's just..." My voice trailed off.

"You're defending him?"

"No! There's nothing to defend."

Nate's eyes narrowed into slits. "Just stay away from him."

Seriously? Nate was getting all territorial on me?

"You can't tell me what to do."

I stormed outside and got into Nate's car, slamming the door. I wouldn't even have gone with him if Willie hadn't been at Nate's house alone with Lucinda (she texted me that she was there), and I didn't trust her anymore.

Nate slammed his door, too, and we suffered through the drive in silence. I just couldn't believe what a jerk he was being. Maybe I should go out with Chase, just to show him he didn't own me.

Nate cranked the stereo up, and I stared out the passenger window. My cheeks burned with anger, and I bit my lip to keep the tears at bay. When we finally pulled into Nate's driveway, I almost ran to his front door. Anything to not have to look at him and talk.

Lucinda pulled away from where she was sitting up close to Willie when she heard the door open.

"Oh, hi, Casey," she said.

"Hey."

"Willie and I were just watching *Days of our Lives*. You should see him blush!"

"Trash TV?" I snapped. "That's the best you can do? What's wrong with PBS?"

"Hey, what's gotten into you?"

Nate finally entered in time to hear that. I tried not to scowl when I said, "Nothing."

Lucinda's lips puckered like she didn't believe that in a million years.

Nate stayed silent and left us in the living room. I settled in a chair across from Willie and Lucinda, tucking my feet in under my rear end.

"Is everything okay?" Willie asked gently.

"Yeah."

"Casey?" Lucinda said in a way that told me she knew I was lying.

"Fine. Nate and I had a fight."

Lucinda's eyes popped wide. "A fight? But you guys never fight. Oh, my goodness. What are you fighting about?"

"Chase Miller. He gave me flowers."

Lucinda gasped. "Holy, love triangle, Batman."

"Batman?" Willie said.

"He's a cartoon." I rolled my eyes. "Nate's being dumb. It's not like I'd go out with the guy."

Lucinda latched on. "Did he ask you?"

I played dumb. "Who?"

She gave me a knowing look. "Chase?"

I shifted in my chair. "Yeah, he asked me out."

Lucinda's face widened with shock. "Does he know that Nate's your boyfriend?"

"Yes, he knows."

"And he *still* asked you out?"

I nodded and bit my cheek. For some reason, I felt like grinning. It's not every day a girl is sought out by two guys.

"Hmm," Lucinda said. "Chase is pretty hot. I can see why Nate's worried."

"Lucinda!" Geez, way to take my side.

25

CASEY

THE TURNER MUSEUM was in the vicinity of the Watson farm, or rather where the Watson farm was in 1862. Now the farm was a strip mall along a busy four lane highway.

The museum portion was in the old farmhouse, which had been restored to its stately nineteenth century manor condition. It was actually better, since electricity and running water had been added.

The wood and brick structure had two stories, with a broad porch and a prominent oak door. There were two white-trimmed gables in the upper floor with lace curtains hanging in the windows.

Willie let out a small gasp. "I was just here, maybe a week ago, when the Turners lived here." He pointed to the nearby fifteen-floor apartment condo building. "There used to be a barn there. We had a send-off dance before we left for the infantry. It's where Timothy enlisted."

It was kind of eerie hearing him talk about Tim like that.

We entered the foyer, which had dark, wood floors and opened to a wide staircase with a red carpet runner.

There were a few pieces of antique furniture, chairs, sofas, lamps, but mostly there were large, black-and-white photographs hanging on the walls or propped up on easels. A number of glass cases contained artifacts from the era.

"That's Mrs. Turner's broach." Willie pointed to a gold-plated leaf with a missing back pin. "She was wearing it at the dance." He shook his head. "And now she's dead."

Long dead.

"Do you need to sit down for a bit?" I motioned to one of the high backed chairs. I could only imagine how over-whelming the last couple days must've been for him.

"No, I'm fine."

I asked the curator where we could find information about the Watson family that resided nearby. She directed us to the former dining room, where the local family records were kept.

Willie had lost color, and I almost insisted he sit. Instead, Lucinda grasped one of his hands. He gripped back tightly.

The dining room was unfurnished, but the elaborate chandelier still hung overhead. A closed up brick fireplace remained in the corner, and over by the window a huge, leather ledger sat opened on a flat-topped pedestal. I started thumbing through it until I got to the Ws.

Nate stepped in beside me. We hadn't said a word to each other since our fight that morning. He'd kept the stereo up loud on the drive over, so it wouldn't have been possible to speak even if we'd wanted to.

I didn't know how this was going to play out. Nate and I'd never fought before, and the thing we were fighting about was so stupid.

Still, we had to put our petty argument aside for Willie, who had far bigger issues.

"Thomas and Anna Watson, of 20561 Farmers Street," I read aloud. "Mr. Watson, born 1814, died..." My eyes shot to Willie. "Not important."

I read off the list of children. "Sara, William, Duncan, Josephine, Michael, Jonathon, Abigail, Maryann, Susan, Daniel..." All had the dates of their births and deaths. I was glad Willie wasn't reading this. In fact his eyes hadn't opened since I'd started.

"Sara Watson married Henry Abernathy." I smiled to myself, remembering how excited she was about her new beau. I was glad to know things worked out for her.

"They had six children." Five lived and one didn't. I kept that info to myself.

I came to Willie's name, which listed his date of birth and death. May 4, 1863. I glanced at Nate whose eyes encouraged me to skip ahead.

"Josephine married a fellow named John Longhorn." Oh good, so my stupid brother didn't ruin her reputation.

"I don't know that name," Willie said. "They must've met, after..."

Were we doing the right thing? How was this supposed to help?

"Uh, yeah," I said. "They had four children."

"Duncan married Alice Clarkson."

"Nice girl," Willie said.

"Do you want me to keep going?"

"I've missed out on it all already. I want to know."

Right. And if he goes back, he'll still miss out on it. Because he dies.

"There's more information beside each name," I said. "Duncan moved into Boston after the war to study law and became a prominent lawyer."

"Abigail won the strawberry pie contest at the summer fair seven years in a row."

I skipped back up the list to read more about Sara. "Henry and Sara Abernathy were married for thirty-five years, farming the family homestead long after the elder Watsons were gone."

"Wow, thirty-five years is a good run," Lucinda said.

Then my eyes landed on the paragraph beside Willie's name, and I froze.

Nate noticed my hesitation. "What is it?"

"Willie, it says here that you are a hero. You gave your life to save another."

His eyes opened and bore into mine.

"You saved Henry Abernathy's life in the war."

26

TIM

FINALLY, it was happening.

We were lined up in a place called Bull's Run. Row upon row upon row, all of us overheating in our crazy blue jackets, loaded down with ammunition, sweat lines dripping down our dirty faces. I spit out the fine Virginia dust that I breathed in through my mouth.

Canons were lined up to our left and right. The Cavalry was spread out between us. We numbered in the thousands, like a small city.

My heart raced as the general rode his horse along the front row, yelling who knew what. I totally understood the need for guys like Joseph now, and I pictured him some-where near the back crapping his pants as he prepared to blow the signal to fire.

My rifle was ready, and I held it up to my shoulder with slippery hands. The Confederate Army was lined up in a similar fashion, maybe a half-mile away, waiting like we were. Everyone was so polite in this war. I wondered who'd be the first to call it.

"This is *déjà vu*," the guy beside me said. "I fought in the first battle of Bull's Run last year. We lost that one. I hope we do better this time."

The *rat-a-tat-tat* of the snare drums reverberated across the meadow and my nerves shot off. The bugle sounded and some poor guy who had the unfortunate job of flag runner sprinted towards the enemy line with nothing but the Union flag in his hand. He was yelling his head off as he went, and I wondered how long it would take for him to be shot dead.

It went from zero to sixty in two seconds flat.

I fired off my musket, and the adrenaline rush almost flattened me. It took so long between shots to reload, I was certain to be hit before I could get off another. The air filled with gunpowder haze, and it burned my nostrils. My heart beat faster than the marching drums. Plumes of smoke rose up in indiscriminate places, and cannon balls landed and exploded, shaking the ground beneath our feet.

Men were yelling and screaming everywhere on both sides–pure chaos. If someone was in charge of this mess, you'd be hard pressed to tell who. Guys were falling to the ground, crying and bloodied. Those who were too close to be shot at were stabbed with bayonets.

I hurried to prep my rifle for another shot, my hand shaking as I poured gunpowder into the barrel, along with the wrapper and musket. I couldn't beat it down with the ramrod fast enough. Right beside me the guy who'd had the *déjà vu* took a bullet to the head. Red drops of blood splattered outward, and his body crumbled to the ground like a heap of dirty laundry.

I shot off another plug, before I could puke, hitting someone who yelled out in agony before falling to the ground. I couldn't be sure it was a Confederate man. The uniforms were too similar in color to tell, and the smoke and gunpowder blast made it hard to see.

James raced by me and I was tempted to grab his arm and pull him back, but his zeal to fight was stronger than my desire to save him.

Everywhere there were bodies on the ground. I pressed forward with the rest of them when another piece of Civil War trivia came to mind.

We lost this one, too.

I stepped over guys on the ground, not wanting to trample on anyone, dead or alive. But especially dead. Casey had been right, this wasn't a game.

I got off another shot just as a man stormed at me, his bayonet aimed at my chest. I dodged him impulsively, the desire to live suddenly loud and strong, but I lost my footing.

Henry came out of nowhere, bursting through the smoke, and impaled my attacker just in time.

"Thanks, man," I said, but he'd already disappeared into the fray again.

I tried to load my gun, but my hands shook too violently. I had to get a grip, or I'd be shot. And there was one thing I was sure of now: I didn't want to die here.

I spotted a familiar form lying in front of me with a leg twisted unnaturally and a red blotch growing on his chest.

James.

I dropped to the ground and crawled to his side to see if he was alive. Just minutes ago he passed me full of passion and drive. Now he lay dead in the mud his gray eyes wide open, staring at nothing.

I turned around to vomit.

I wiped my mouth on my sleeve and then got to work reloading my rifle. I pulled myself to my feet, but my legs felt like rubber. My tongue was like a thick cotton ball in my mouth and I knew I was dehydrated. I couldn't even tell what direction to shoot. Before I could regain my bearings, immense pain exploded in my leg, and I fell to the ground.

I yelled out as I pulled off my belt. I was smart enough to know that I needed to stop the flow of blood if I didn't want to bleed to death and that it had to be done before I passed out.

I pulled it tight above the wound, crying openly. For the first time I considered that defying Casey back at Camp Cameron was the stupidest thing I'd ever done and that maybe her theory was wrong. I might actually die here.

The thought terrified me.

27

CASEY

WE WERE BACK at Nate's with our newfound information, which he took to his room to help in the search online. I sat in the living room with Willie and Lucinda feeling like the third wheel. Things were still weird between Nate and me, but I didn't have the emotional energy to get into it with him right now.

The front door creaked open, and Mrs. Mackenzie walked in.

"Hi, there," she said with her mouth, but her eyes said. "Why are there so many kids in my house?"

"Hi, Mrs. Mackenzie." I moved my feet out from under my butt. "We're just waiting for Nate."

She nodded and set her purse and briefcase on the table before going to the kitchen. Nate's mom wore a suit jacket over a pencil skirt that ended at her knees and stilettos. Her dark hair was salon-styled around her heart-shaped face and she had trendy glasses perched on her nose. You could see where Nate got his good looks from.

We heard cupboards and drawers open and close in the kitchen and the sound of the espresso machine steaming milk.

"Maybe we should get out of her way," I said.

Willie and Lucinda followed me to Nate's room. He didn't move from his computer desk when we piled in and sat in a row like three monkeys on the edge of his bed. Hear no evil, see no evil, speak no evil.

It was awkward to say the least.

Nate turned to us, but he didn't look anyone in the eye. "I've been working on a heritage site."

"Did you find anything?" I asked.

"The Turner museum only recorded three generations of the Watson family line. Samuel said we had to find out if anything would change if Willie stayed."

"We already know that Henry will die if I don't go back," Willie said.

"Not necessarily," I said. "It's possible that someone else could've been there to save him if you weren't. We don't really know the circumstances of that situation."

"Okay, here's Willie's family." Nate pointed to his computer screen. "I'm starting with Sara and Henry's lineage."

Nate tapped away on his keyboard and I stood to peer over him. I could smell Nate's cologne, and if we weren't in the middle of this stupid fight, I was pretty sure I would've shoved my face into his neck. He shifted in his seat.

"This could take a few minutes."

Gotcha. I backed up and distracted myself by staring at the posters of all Nate's sports heroes. It was either that or gag at the way Lucinda and Willie made eyes at each other.

The Tom Brady poster was the largest, and my eyes darted to the flattened ball that lay on the trophy shelf nearby. The ball that started it all with Nate and me. If I hadn't jumped up spontaneously to catch an overthrow by Tyson that day Lucinda and I stayed after school to watch the practice (or more accurately, watch the hot guys and specifically Nate), none of this would've happened.

I walked across his room and picked it up, running my fingers against the hole in the middle of Tom Brady's signature. I remembered the horror I felt when some upstart from the past missed the squirrel he was aiming at and hit Nate's football instead.

So much had happened since then, it felt like another lifetime ago.

Nate swiveled to look at us. "I'm done. There are a few gaps, but I was able to identify one living relative, still in the Cambridge area. A Clarice Watson. Married name, Porter."

I carefully placed Nate's ball back on the shelf.

"Clarice Porter? That's the same name as the cop who saved Tim's life."

Willie crumbled a little. "Sara and Henry's great, great, great, granddaughter, saved Tim's life?"

I put a hand on his shoulder. "A cosmic coincidence?"

Nate's fingers kept clicking on his keyboard. Then he turned to us. "I can't find anyone else in this area with the same name."

"So?" I prompted.

"Well, I'm no physicist," Nate said, "but what happens when the date of the day Willie saves Henry's life passes in the past and Henry dies. His whole ancestry would be erased, right?

I shook my head at the catastrophic possibility. "Talk about a huge butterfly."

"I'm confused," Willie said. "What do butterflies have to do with anything?"

"It's this theory that a butterfly flapping its wings in the Amazonian rain forest could cause a ripple effect in the universe that would create a tsunami on the other side of the world. Basically, every little thing that happens has a big effect elsewhere at another time in the future."

Willie's jaw went slack. "And I'm the butterfly?"

My heart sank. "I guess you could say that."

Willie closed his eyes and let out a long breath. "That settles it then," he said. "I have to go back. I have to save Henry. I have to save Tim. I have to save the world."

It sounded dramatic but it could be true.

Or not.

"Maybe Nate's right and someone else will save Henry," Lucinda said. "We can't give up on Willie's life so easily. There must be someone else there, right? Because you're not?"

"But what if we're wrong?" Willie said, looking at her. "What if no one else is there to save him? Then poof! Sara's whole lineage disappears. Including Officer Porter."

"We don't know if that would happen," I insisted.

Willie's eyes settled on me. "We don't know that it won't."

Was Officer Porter the only one who could've saved Tim? And if Willie didn't go back, would Officer Porter really cease to exist?

The whole thing was giving me a headache.

Willie hid his face in his hands. "As much as I don't want to die," he said through his fingers, "I can't take a chance with the outcome. I have to go back."

"Oh, Willie." Lucinda, burst into tears.

Then she leaned into him and kissed him on the lips. Instead of closing his eyes like most people do while kissing, Willie's eyes grew wide, and I wondered if he'd ever been kissed before.

I turned my back to them, to give them a little privacy. I felt for Willie. If he went back, he'd die and miss out on his chance to experience what it was like to fall in love, to raise a family, to make his mark in the world.

On the other hand, if he didn't go back, Sara would miss out on those things, not to mention that Henry would miss out, too.

Nate raised his eyebrows at the make-out scene on his bed.

His eyes came back to me. "You need to see this."

I thought he'd come up with a solution to Willie's dilemma so I grabbed Willie's hand. "Break it up, you two."

I pulled Willie over to look at Nate's laptop. He'd found another Civil War site and had been browsing through old black-and-white photos.

"What's this?"

"I came across this site yesterday, and I thought I should show it to you. These are photos of soldiers in the Union army, Willie's regiment, the 13th Mass. Photography was getting a good foothold during that era, just in time to record quite a lot of the war and the men in it."

A shot of fear tingled my spine. "And..."

"I just found this."

Nate clicked on an icon he'd shrunk at the bottom of the screen. It opened up, and there in front of us, in his Union army uniform was Tim.

I felt like I couldn't breathe. "What does it say? Did he die?"

Before Nate could answer me, my head started spinning. I already had Willie's hand and just in time I grabbed Nate's arm. The three of us tumbled through the spiral of light, and we all landed with a thud on the ground surrounded by tall trees blowing wildly in the wind.

28

CASEY

A RUSH OF WIND blew my hair into my eyes. I fell to my back in an exhausted heap staring up at the blue sky. Tall trees thick with a canopy of leaves swayed overhead like giant upside-down brooms, sunlight pushing through with long fingers of light.

Despite the wind, my ears became attuned to the presence of forest noises–bugs and birds, squirrels and foxes–and the absence of car engines, TV chatter, background music, and air traffic.

Willie looked like someone had slapped him across the face.

"Are you okay?" I asked him.

His head slowly bobbed. "Are we really back? My parents, my family, alive?"

I forced myself to sit up. "Yes and yes."

"Do you know where we are?" Nate asked.

I'd never tripped from his house before and he lived a good ten minutes away from me by car.

"Not exactly," I said.

"I've got to get home," Willie said. "I need to see my family. And then..."

And then re-enlist. I wondered what kind of punishment they'd hand out. But if the history we read about in the library remained true, he did in fact get re-enlisted. Probably due to the shortage of soldiers. No sense keeping an able-bodied person locked up behind bars.

Willie started walking, pushing through forest brush and Nate and I stepped in behind him. Eventually, we hit a dirt road, more of a horse path, really. We followed it until we came upon a highway marker.

"I know where we are now," Willie said.

"Great." I pulled out small twigs and leaves that had gotten caught in my hair. "We have to do something about our clothes when we can."

Willie took the lead. "We have plenty at home."

He did indeed know the way to his farm, and we circled in the back way on the same path Josephine and I had used to sneak out on our doomed horseback ride to retrieve Tim. When I thought of him in that old Union army photograph I felt a weird mix of pride and fear, and extreme annoyance. What a brat!

I just hoped he was able to stay out of trouble, and by trouble I meant not lying dead in some field. I had Nate with me now, so if we had to pin him down forcibly to get him home, we would do it.

We stopped by the water pump, taking turns scooping up water to soothe our parched throats.

"What's the plan?" Nate asked.

Before we could answer, another voice interrupted. "Willie?"

"Josephine!" Willie ran to his sister, and twirled her in an emotional hug.

"Oh, good Lord, Willie! Do you know how much trouble you're in?" Josephine backed away and took a long look at her brother, wiping tears from her eyes. "I'm just so glad you're alive."

Then she saw our clothes. "And what on earth are you all wearing?"

"Is the family okay?" Willie asked, ignoring her question.

"Well, we'd been told you defected. A collection of soldiers came and searched the whole house and property. We didn't believe them, of course. We were sure that something horrible must've happened to you. Ma's in a dreadful state."

"I'm so sorry," he said.

"What happened to you, then? There was also talk that you'd gotten very ill and in a state of delusion, wandered off the base and got lost in the forest to be eaten by wild animals."

"Josephine," I said, needing to get us back on track. "I know you are a great keeper of confidences..."

Her eyes lit up and she nodded.

"We promise to explain everything later, but first, do you think you could get us some clothes and meet us at the cabin?"

"I can't wait to hear this one," she said leaving us alone to work on a story.

"What are we going to tell her?" Willie said.

We kept ourselves shielded by the trees at the edge of the property as we made our way to the back side of the cabin where we waited for Josephine.

"That's not a bad idea," I said. "About you being ill. If we go with that one, then the army might go easier on what punishment they choose."

"I suppose it's as good as any," he agreed. "And I really don't want to go down in history as a defector."

I smiled at him. "I don't remember reading anything like that about you."

We heard Josephine's hushed voice, calling, "Willie."

"We're behind the cabin," he called back softly.

We took the clothing Josephine handed to us. "So?"

Willie kept to the story about being ill, and somehow by the time he was finished, Nate and I happened to have found him lying in the forest almost dead.

Josephine's forehead wrinkled up.

"I'm confused," she said. "I thought Nathaniel had enlisted in Springfield. Did you defect, too. And Cassandra, why are you dressed so wantonly?"

Nate and Willie looked at me with cocked eyebrows, waiting for what kind of story I would concoct now.

"Um, well, the thing is Josephine, we're from a poor family, and so sometimes, uh, Nate, uh, Nathaniel and I..." What? What do we do? Then it hit me. I added with a rush, "... join a Vaudeville show."

"A Vaudeville show?" Josephine's eyes brightened with curiosity. "What is that?"

"It's entertainment. You know, singing and dancing and acting. We take it on the road, from village to village."

Oh, the tangled web we weave.

"But, why haven't I heard of it? Do you perform in Boston?"

Nate broke in. "It's not very good. We're not proud of it, so we don't tell our friends. But we really do have to get going."

"Yes," I said, agreeing. "I'm going to sneak into the cabin to change."

I changed into the dress Josephine brought for me as quickly as possible, wanting to get moving on our quest to find Tim.

When I got back to the guys, they were already changed. Josephine had left to give them privacy.

We stood awkwardly, staring, knowing that we needed to say goodbye, and that we'd never see Willie again.

"Cassandra and Nathaniel," Willie said, reverting back to our nineteenth century titles. "It's been an extreme honor and a pleasure."

"For us as well." My eyes started swelling along with my throat and there was no way I could keep the waterworks at bay.

I studied Willie's blue eyes lined with golden lashes, the way his pale skin was sprinkled with freckles, and how his copper curls hung on his forehead.

No wonder Lucinda fell hard and fast.

It was like he read my mind.

"Tell Lucinda I'm sorry I didn't have a chance to say a proper goodbye. She's a beautiful girl, and I'm very glad to have met her."

"I will, Willie."

Nate reached out his hand. "You're a good man."

I threw myself at Willie, not caring at all about nineteenth century protocol and squeezed him hard. "Goodbye, Willie."

I COULDN'T HOLD my sobs back as we walked through the growing darkness toward Boston. I wiped my nose on the back of my dress sleeve, not caring at all how unattractive I must've been.

It was the first time Nate and I had been alone since our fight. His jaw worked as he walked, and I wondered what he was thinking. I lifted my skirts in an effort to keep up to his long strides, wondering if he was waiting for me to apologize. But for what? I never did anything wrong. He was the one who got his knickers in a knot over Chase and his flowers, making it into this big ugly thing. He was the one who should apologize.

We heard the clip-clop of horses and the rattle of a carriage coming from behind. Nate pulled me off the road to hide behind a clump of trees until it passed by, and then we both ran after it. With one hand pulling up my skirt, I followed as we jumped on the back bumper. Stowaway skills were a must for my line of work.

Thankfully it was dusk, and the road was empty with the exception of this carriage. Our freeloading went unnoticed. Unfortunately, carriages in this time didn't come with shock-absorbing suspension, and by the time we were pulled over the bridge, my body was fully shaken. Men were lighting the oil lamps that lined sections of main roads so when Nate and I hopped off, we had to take extra care to keep to the shadows.

"We need to find the army base," I said.

Nate shook his head. "Tim won't be there."

"How do you know?"

"It's August 29th. The 13th Massachusetts is at Bull Run."

"How do you know this?"

Nate turned his head and shrugged. "I've become a student of nineteenth century history recently, specializing in the years leading up to and including the Civil War. For obvious reasons."

He'd been doing his homework.

He softened his voice and continued, "The first day of fighting has already happened."

I felt my knees give out. "We're too late?"

He paused. "I don't know."

"There's another day of battle tomorrow," he added. "We need to get to Virginia."

Right. But how to do that with no money and not enough time?

"As lovely as you are in that nightgown, Casey," Nate's eyes settled on me, "I'm wondering if it's the right look for what we need to do next."

I lowered my voice. "You think I need to go back to *Mr. Casey*?"

Nate smirked. "It would be to your own benefit, but I think you're going to find it harder to pull off."

"I can kill the wiggle."

His smirk reached his eyes. "But you can't kill the curves."

I felt a blush forming and suppressed a giggle. It'd been a while since we'd engaged in playful bantering and it made me feel good. Maybe our fight was over, just fizzled out like a popped balloon.

"I'd be more comfortable in pants anyway," I said. "You got a plan?"

"As much as I hate to do it," Nate pointed to a clothes line on a nearby property and took off before I could say anything. He unpinned a pair of trousers and a shirt. After I'd changed, I made him go back and pin my dress on the line in exchange.

"Here's a cap," Nate said, handing me one he'd swiped off the rocker on the front porch.

I twisted my hair into a knot on the top of my head and pulled the hat on.

"The train station is in the south end," I said.

"We'll have to hop it," Nate said, as we started walking.

My heart skipped at the thought. I'd jumped a few carriages in my time, but hopping a train was a whole other thing. They were bigger and faster for starters, but I didn't have a choice. I had to do it if I wanted to find Tim. So we crouched in the bushes waiting for the next Baltimore and Ohio train headed south to Virginia.

"The Confederates blew up a number of bridges on this line," Nate said. "The Feds have fixed some of them, but it doesn't go as far as it used to."

I suddenly felt like the student here. I was sure I'd read about this somewhere along the way, but I'd forgotten.

I heard the whistle, and my heart started pounding. I imagined losing my footing and getting sucked underneath and sliced in two. Not a pretty picture.

"It looks fairly simple in the movies," Nate said, trying to reassure me.

"The movies make everything seem simple."

"Ready?"

I nodded and swallowed hard. The *chug, chug* of the steam engine grew louder. At least steam-drawn trains were slow compared to their modern counterparts.

When it reached us we started running. Nate grabbed onto a ladder that ran down the side of one of the cars.

"Run, Casey! Take my hand!"

I wasn't much of a sprinter, but I pushed my long legs as hard as they would go. For a moment I freaked, thinking I'd miss Nate's hand, and we'd be separated again. But in the last second I felt his strong grip, and my feet left the ground, landing finally on a lower rung.

I felt like laughing and crying.

Nate wedged the car door open and pulled me inside. It was dark and loaded with boxed supplies heading for the front.

I dropped to the floor of the car and rolled on my back. It took me a long moment to catch my breath.

"We did it," I finally said.

Nate crawled over and lay beside me. It felt good to feel the warmth of his bare arm against mine. "That's something I never thought I'd do in my lifetime," he said.

I turned to face him, holding his gaze. "I'm glad you're with me."

He threaded his arm under my head. We both smelled bad and looked less than optimal, and lying on the hard bumping surface of the car floor was nowhere close to romantic, but it was comforting all the same.

He squeezed my hand and kissed me lightly on the lips. "I'm glad, too."

Our fight was officially over, for now. We hadn't worked anything out, but it was obvious by Nate's posture that he'd called a truce. As long as Chase lived next door, there could be tension between us over it, but we weren't there right now. And I didn't want to think about Chase anymore. We were soothed by the rocking rhythm of the train, and even though I hadn't meant to close my eyes, I fell asleep.

I AWOKE IN THE MORNING, dying of thirst and starving to death. Yeah, *death and dying* were not the best adjectives to use when you were on a train taking you to a war zone. The nice thing was I woke up with Nate's arm stretched over me. I hated to lift it off, but I wanted to dig through the packages on the train now that enough daylight shone through the slits in the wood for us to see.

Mostly I found ammunition. Crate after crate of gunpowder and bullets and I worried that we'd be eating explosives for breakfast. Then I came across a crate full of crackers. I grabbed one and took a bite and almost broke a tooth.

"What the heck?"

"What's going on?" Nate's sleepy voice carried across the box car.

"I'm looking for food."

I saw him sit up and rub his neck in the half-light. "Find anything?"

"Some kind of rock hard cracker."

"I read about those," he said. "Hard tack. Tasteless but last forever."

I handed him one. "Better start gumming."

I kept digging, hoping to find bottled water somewhere, but no such luck. "Water must be in another car."

"I imagine we'll be stopping soon," Nate said, still working his cracker. "We'll have to jump off and disappear before anyone sees us."

I sat against a crate and dug into my cracker. The rocking of the car rubbed the edge of the crate into my shoulder blade. I shifted, trying to find a more comfortable position.

"We could've checked," Nate said. "You know, if we'd had time."

"Checked what?"

"On Tim. Online."

Oh. If he'd died here or not, for sure. They obviously had a record of a Timothy Donovan, if that picture was to prove anything.

"There's still time to find him and get him home." Right? I refused to believe anything else.

"Sure," he said, but he diverted his eyes from mine.

My heart stalled at the notion that Nate might be doubtful, but I didn't challenge him.

He'd taken time recently to check on the stats.

"How many casualties?" I asked.

His eyes darted up to catch mine. "What?"

"How many soldiers died in this battle?"

His eyes dropped back to his cracker.

"Nate?"

"A lot."

A lot? "How many?"

He swallowed, nearly gagging on cracker bits. "Over thirteen thousand Union soldiers."

A dark, syrupy fear spread through my body. "That's a lot." Was Tim among them?

Nate was right about us stopping soon, and it wasn't long before the train started to slow. Nate cracked the side door open. "Ready?"

I followed him out onto the ladder, hanging on tight. The force of the wind whipped our faces and the grassy green of the ground blurred beneath us. As soon as the train was slow enough we jumped off and rolled into the weeds.

I shouted out in pain.

"Casey!"

"It's okay." I breathed through the throbbing. "I just landed on my shoulder wrong."

"We need to get out of view." Nate lifted me up, and I winced.

We stayed low and scrambled into the trees as far away from the train as we could. I leaned up against the white bark of a birch tree.

"Casey?" Nate eyed me with concern.

"I'm fine." I had to be fine. We were running out of time. "It's just a bruise."

We hiked until we came across a little stream where we both dropped to our knees and scooped water into our mouths.

"I think we're in Virginia," Nate said after he'd had his fill.

I followed his gaze where it landed on a road marker to our right. *Richmond 50* was carved into the side.

"Fifty miles?" I said.

"We don't have to get to Richmond."

Nate splashed his face with water and pulled the bottom of his shirt up to dry it. I refused to let his six-pack distract me.

"How long will that take us to walk?" I said, drying my own face.

"If we average three miles an hour, about fifteen hours."

I pulled myself to my feet. "We better get going then."

29

TIM

TIMMM-OTHH-YYY.

I heard my name. It sounded tinny and stretched out like it was coming from the other side of a long tunnel.

Ow.

My cheeks burned, first one then the other, accompanied by a slapping sound. I heard a groan leave my dry, cracked lips.

"Timothy, thank God you're alive."

My eyelids stuck to my eyeballs and scratched like sandpaper. I couldn't see the owner of the voice.

I was too stiff to move, like a dried up twig with no give. Someone poured water in my mouth. I was aware of my head being lifted so I could drink, but my only focus was to swallow hard and fast.

"Easy, you don't want to choke."

I knew the voice now.

"Joseph?" It came out thick like I had a sock in my mouth.

"Yeah, it's me."

I flopped back to the ground and now that I was conscious, my body shot all its messages to me at once. Flames ran up my left leg.

"My leg," I groaned, through gritted teeth.

"You've been shot. It looks bad." Then he yelled over my head. "Over here! Another one over here!"

I mumbled, "I thought you fainted at the sight of blood?"

Joseph shrugged. "I'm getting used to it. Good thing or I'd be fainting every two minutes."

"What's happening?" The words felt like marbles in my mouth.

"The battle's moved south and is winding down." Joseph's eyes scanned the landscape. "We're picking up our dead and wounded."

"How long have I been out?"

"Since yesterday, I imagine. You didn't come back to camp last night. We thought we lost you, too."

Too? My chest constricted as I remembered James.

"James is gone," I whispered.

Joseph confirmed it by nodding. I barely recognized his face with all the dirt and grime smeared over it. His eyes were just a couple of white orbs staring at me through the dimming daylight.

I heard the clip-clopping of horses as they drew beside me, a three-wheeled wagon like a large, wooden wheelbarrow, pulled up behind them.

Two guys appeared and lifted me onto a makeshift gurney, and I yelled out in pain. I was the third man on the cart, filling it to capacity.

I had no idea where they were taking us. I pushed my eyes shut trying to beat back the pain. I saw Joseph's face in my mind's eye and realized I'd forgotten to thank him.

Us guys in the back of the cart groaned and moaned in three-part harmony. Eventually, we pulled up beside a no-nonsense, two-story, red sandstone house.

The stone house should have a no-vacancy sign in the window. Every bit of floor space was packed with injured men like a tin of sardines. I wondered what the owners thought of this takeover.

We were given water that came from a well on the property and those stupid hard tack crackers for those of us conscious enough to eat. One of the doctors made rounds in the room, assessing the injuries. He was hardly able to hide how overwhelmed he felt.

Every once in a while a man would grow quiet and still. A doctor would push the eyelids closed if they weren't already and call for someone to carry the corpse out.

The floor underneath me was hard and unforgiving, and I imagined bedsores would soon be forming on my rear end. Even though it was evening, the room was stifling hot, or maybe I was burning up from within. Sweat ran off my brow into my eyes. I couldn't remember the last time I'd showered, and I wasn't the only one. The stone house reeked of perspiration and festering wounds.

Flies and mosquitoes found their way through the open doors and windows, but I was too weak to swat them away from my throbbing leg. My bullet wound had grown angrier since my arrival here. Pink and oozing pus. Burning red lines sprouting like the sun. Hadn't these people heard of disinfectant?

"Hey doc," I called with a raspy voice to one of the guys in a white cloak.

He stepped over. "Son?"

"Got something for the pain? And how about some

Polysporin?"

He eyed me with a confused look. "I'm afraid I'm all out of whiskey, but it should be arriving soon."

"As much as I'd like a drink..."

"It's for your wound, son. Not to drink."

The doctor left me with the sound of my own uneven breathing rushing my ears.

"You gotta girl?"

I turned my head to face the cracking voice. His cheeks glistened with sweat and he held a grimy hand over a patch of blood growing on his chest. I guessed him to be in his early twenties. He lay next to me in the corner, so close we were almost touching.

"Nah," I said.

I thought briefly of Josie, but she was something fun in passing. Like any girl I'd hook up with at a party at home.

"I do." The guy tried to smile, but grimaced instead with pain. "Sally's her name. We're getting married."

I'd never been in love, but I realized suddenly I wanted to be. Shallow relationships seemed so stupid to me now that I lay in a row left to die. My chest felt heavy with regret. I'd treated my family so poorly, and now I felt certain I'd never see them again. A hard lump formed in my throat.

"She's real sweet," the guy said.

Those were his last words. His eyes stared blankly past me and his chest stopped moving.

I caught my own breath. The world paused in our little corner.

I lay beside the dead man for a good ten minutes before a couple of war-weary soldiers picked him up and took him away.

I wished I'd at least asked him his name.

30

CASEY

NATE AND I HAD GONE a whole year without a fight, and now it seemed we couldn't go a whole day.

Maybe it was because we were both stressed and exhausted, overheated and dehydrated. Or maybe it was just because.

I'd stopped to pick some wild flowers. We'd been marching for hours without a break except for water in the creek we were following. My subconscious must've longed for a diversion, something beautiful and peaceful.

"What are you doing?" Nate said incredulously when he saw the small bouquet in my hand. "Despite what the idiom says, we don't have time to stop to smell the roses."

I knew that. I *knew* that. It *was* my brother we were trying to find, after all.

"They make me feel better," I pouted.

"I don't get why girls like flowers so much. They just die after a couple of days."

Were we talking about flowers or Chase now?

"It was a nice gesture," I said with my nose up in the air. "You're just mad you didn't do it first."

"Do what first?"

I turned and stared him down. "Give me flowers first."

"Is that what this is about? Chase Miller?"

Okay, I'd admit it. It bugged me that Nate never thought to bring me flowers and Chase did. "I'm not making it about him."

He flashed me a withering look. "You're the one who said it was a nice gesture."

"It *was* a nice gesture."

"What? You want flowers? *Flowers* are a nice gesture?" He threw his arms wide. "What about this? I'm *here* aren't I? How's that for a nice gesture?"

My heart squeezed with a searing pain. I felt my eyes well up. I turned away, not wanting him to see how much he'd just hurt me. He was *here* out of obligation and some twisted sense of duty, not love. Not like before.

"Casey." He reached for me, but I pulled away.

I didn't want to look at him, and I definitely didn't want him touching me.

Hot, angry tears streamed down my face. I mopped them off with the back of my hand leaving a smudge of dirt. Great. My face was a dusty, tear dribbled mess and I didn't need a mirror to know I looked like crap.

We trudged forward in tense, stilted silence that was thick like the mud along the creek bank. The heat of the sun beating down on my head only fueled the furnace of hurt in my heart.

"Casey..." Nate tried again.

"Are we even going the right way?" I interrupted, refusing to look at him.

He sighed. "I think so. We're still heading south."

The silence between us was loud. I just wanted it all to end. Find Tim, go home. Finished. Eventually, we stopped at a spot where the creek pooled, to drink and wash our faces. The cold water on my hot skin sizzled, making me gasp.

Then I dipped a hard cracker/food thing in the water to soften it up. I didn't feel like eating, but I knew I had to keep my strength up.

I sneaked a peek at Nate. He'd dunked his head in the creek and water ran down his back as he shook his hair out, sealing his cotton shirt to his athletic, broad shoulders. His mouth no longer turned up in a sensual smile when he looked back at me. Instead it stayed in a firm line of determination. Complete the task at hand. Get in, get out.

A lump formed in my throat, and I pushed back tears again as I swallowed more pain. How did we get this way? Just last week we were crazy about each other, and today... I felt like I didn't even know him.

He stood. "We should go."

I pulled myself up and brushed dirt off of my pants, not that it helped with how I looked. I had to push my own troubles away for now, my heartache and my vanity, and focus on finding my brother.

The orange hue of the sun cast long shadows as it set. We still hadn't found Tim, and the second day of battle was now over. We were too late.

Panic squished me, and I felt short of breath. I almost fell to my knees in grief when Nate pointed.

Just over the hill, pillars of smoke.

We started to run.

"Wait!" Nate reached for me, pulling me to a stop. "They might shoot at us."

He broke a branch off a nearby tree. Then he unbuttoned his shirt and peeled it off, tying the sleeves to the branch to fashion a makeshift surrender flag.

I'd surrender at the sight of his bare chest and the way his biceps bulged.

Casey! I was so easily distracted.

Nate jogged ahead. "Stay behind me."

It was nice to know he didn't want me to get shot at. Not on his watch, anyway.

I was relieved to see the Union flag fluttering weakly in the humidity and a crowd of soldiers sitting around small fire pits. Someone pointed when he spotted us, and one of them stood to greet us.

He got straight to the point.

"It's not safe here for civilians."

"We're looking for my brother," I gasped, still catching my breath from the run. Nate detached his shirt from the stick and put it back on.

"If he's not dead, he's not free to go."

I gulped.

Nate said, "We just need to find him. Family emergency. His name is Timothy Donovan."

The man shouted to the crowd. "Anyone know of a Private Timothy Donovan?"

Everyone in hearing distance shook their heads. I couldn't help but noticed how drawn and defeated they all looked. Skinny and bull whipped.

"What about the others?" I said. "The ones who can't hear you?"

The soldier shrugged. "Feel free to ask for yourself."

Nate and I spread out asking every grimy, dazed face we could find, "Do you know Timothy Donovan?"

It was a sea of blue coats and sullen expressions.

Just when I was about to break down and cry, a soldier with dark hair and soft eyes, waved us over. He had a small *New Testament* in his hand.

"I know him," he said.

"Where is he?"

"He was wounded in yesterday's battle."

Icy fear pricked my heart. "He's not..."

"He's alive," another soldier said. He was pretzel thin and one of the few beardless faces there. He looked like a child, not a man, and I couldn't believe anyone would let him join the army much less fight. "I found him on the field myself."

"Where is he?"

"They took him to the Stone House," he pointed. "Down on Sudley-Manassas Road."

31

TIM

THE GUY NEXT TO ME was having a nightmare. I reached over to nudge his shoulder and he shouted out as he woke up.

"Are you okay, man?"

The guy had two heads. That could be why he was shouting. As my eyes scanned the room, I saw two of every-thing–two paintings of a framed landscape, two chandeliers hanging from the center of the room, a lot of identical twins lying on the floor.

The two-headed guy next to me mumbled, and I thought he must be talking in his sleep. He was praying, making some kind of promise to be a better husband and father if God would let him live.

And I would be a better son and brother.

I felt a sob build in my throat, very unsoldier-like. I'd screwed up bad. There was no way I'd find my way back to the Watsons now; no way that Casey would find me. I'd made it virtually impossible.

So stupid!

I didn't want to die here. *I didn't want to die.*

Double vision came with a headache that provided a slight distraction from the screaming in my leg. I joined in the chorus of groans coming from the men around me.

A white cloak, (two, if I were to believe my sight) towered overhead. "Another one over here," the voice said.

Then he bent down. "Son, your leg's no good. We're sending you to the Sudley Church for surgery."

Surgery? My mind felt like fuzz, but I knew enough to know that operations in the nineteenth century, especially ones not in an actual hospital, were something to be avoided.

"No," I said. I barely recognized my own voice; it had grown so thin and weak "Please."

"It'll be all right," the man said. "Better your leg gone than your life."

No!

32

CASEY

THE STONE HOUSE was only a few miles away, and after the long day's hike you'd think I'd have to drag myself the distance. But the thought of finally reaching Tim was the shot of adrenaline I needed.

The sky had grown murky gray, and all we had was the light of the moon. I stumbled on the un-even ground, with a yell.

"Are you okay?" Nate said, reaching for me.

"Yeah, I'm fine." I accepted his hand as he lifted me back to my feet, and we kept moving, totally ignoring the scrapes on my palms.

A flag attached to a two story building flickered in the distance.

"There it is," I said.

My legs seemed to take off without me and I would've tumbled again if I hadn't grabbed onto Nate's arm.

The yard had horses tied to posts and carriages parked to the side. There was another parked by the front door that had just arrived with more wounded soldiers. Other soldiers carried the men into the house one by one. I couldn't help craning my neck to see if any of them were Tim.

We followed them inside and were accosted by a foul stench. Unwashed soldiers, sickness. Death.

A man approached us. "What are you doing here?"

"Please," I said, "we're looking for my brother. We've heard he was wounded in yesterday's battle. We want to take him home."

The man's stern expression softened. I took that as a sign to continue my plea. "He's six feet tall, thin, shaggy brown hair."

"That describes most of the men in this room." He sighed. "Go on in, look around, but be quick about it."

I figured he was happy to unload a wounded soldier. No good to the army now, anyway.

All the furniture had been removed or pushed aside, but photographs and paintings on the walls said this was actually a family home when people weren't shooting at it.

Injured men were lying on every square inch of the bare, hardwood floor. Low moans and sporadic coughing were the only signs of life. Some had their hands over chest wounds; others had limbs wrapped, blood seeping through dirty bandages. All were in some form of agony. The sight made me gag. I tried not to focus on the gruesomeness and the suffering around me, keeping my thoughts on finding Tim.

I muttered, "He must be in here somewhere."

It felt heartless to step over men in such obvious need, but I forced myself to examine faces only, desperate to find Tim's.

The stench that floated up was choking, and Nate and I covered our noses with our shirts.

"Brutal," he said.

Uninjured soldiers moved the patients about like checker pieces–ones with injuries that weren't life-threatening, ones who needed immediate medical attention, ones who were already dead and ready to be moved out.

None were Tim.

"Where *is* he?" I said.

Nate approached one of the doctors. "Are the wounded taken anywhere else?"

The doctor shook his head. "There are more men in the cellar and some upstairs. Who are you looking for?"

"My brother," I said. "Timothy Donovan."

"I recognize the name." He pushed his round-lensed spectacles up on his nose. "It was my responsibility to collect the names of all the men who arrived here and to register the degree of injury. Yes, Timothy Donovan. He had a very bad leg."

Had? "Had?" I whimpered.

"I'm afraid the ambulance has taken him to Sudley Church."

Oh my God. "He *died?*"

"Oh no, my dear. Sudley Church is the field hospital. Your brother has been sent there for surgery."

Surgery! My heart beat like a rabbit's.

"Nate, we have to get him!"

I sprinted toward the door as fast as a person could sprint in a room crowded with sick men all over the floor.

Outside, I grabbed Nate's arm. "What are we going to do? We have to get to him before they operate. This is *1862*. Medicine is archaic!"

Nate took my hand. "Come with me." We stumbled

through the darkness until we reached a horse tied to the furthest post.

"We're stealing a horse?"

"You have a better idea?"

No, I didn't. Besides, the horse would probably come straight back once we let it loose at the church.

I pressed my cheek into the back of Nate's shirt, hanging on for dear life as he heeled the horse's flanks to gallop as fast as it could down the dirt road in the darkness.

My emotions were all over the map. Fear for Tim, heartache for Nate. Even though my arms clung tight around his waist and my body was pressed into his, I'd never felt further away.

The little, white church glowed like a firefly in the moonlight. Soldiers carried men in and out the double front doors, much in the same manner as at the Stone house.

The horse neighed as we cantered to a stop. Nate helped me down, and we sprinted up the stone steps.

"Can I help you?" A woman said.

She wore a long, cotton skirt with her hair tucked under a white bonnet. She had dark circles under worried eyes. No one got any sleep these days.

"Are you a nurse?" I asked. She nodded.

"I'm looking for my brother, Timothy Donovan."

"The boy with the leg wound?"

"Yes, where is he?"

"He's in the back room." The nurse touched my arm and looked gravely into my eyes. "I'm afraid he's about to have it removed."

No, no, no!

Nate and I sprinted to the back of the church, past other

patients on short benches and pews, awaiting their turn for bad medicine.

I heard him before I saw him. Tim's voice crying out, "No, please, don't!" It echoed through the wooden beamed ceiling of the sanctuary.

I threw open the door and nearly fainted. "Stop!"

I freaked out at the sight of archaic surgical tools on the small table beside Tim's gurney. His leg was bare up to the groin, and a gruesome, raw and bloody wound was just above his knee. This was before penicillin, and an injury that could be successfully treated in modern times required a hacksaw in 1862.

"I'm his sister," I said to the startled doctor, totally forgetting about my attempt to disguise myself as a man. "Can we have a minute?"

The doctor frowned, his eyes scanning my attire with disdain. Then he muttered through thin lips. "Make it quick. Can't you see how busy we are? I haven't slept in three days."

He left us alone, but I heard him mumbling something about meddling, misguided women on his way out.

"Tim." I leaned over his cot and took his clammy hand in mine. "I'm so glad we finally found you."

Tim managed a weak grin. "Me, too. I'm kind of fond of my leg." His forehead glistened with sweat and I could feel the heat of his fever rise to my face.

"I'm such an idiot, Casey. I'm sorry."

"Shh, it's okay."

I stared at the green ooze on Tim's exposed leg and imagined the horrible experience he would've gone through if we'd arrived even a few minutes later. It made me nauseous and light headed. It occurred to me that I'd subconsciously worried I would shoot back to the present too soon, and now that we'd finally found Tim, I gave myself permission to give into the dizziness and white light I felt coming on.

I took Nate's arm with one hand and Tim's with the other. "Hold on, boys. We're going home."

33

CASEY

TIM TOPPLED AWKWARDLY onto Nate's bed, letting out an agonizing groan as he fell.

Lucinda screamed. In her timeline, Willie disappeared into thin air, and Tim was suddenly in his place, bloodied and filthy.

Nate snapped up his cell from his desk. "I'm calling 911."

"Tim?" I shook his shoulder. His eyelids fluttered as he moaned, delirious with fever.

Lucinda's head whipped around as she took in the scene, her hands flailing. "Willie's gone?"

"I'm sorry," I said, touching her shoulder. "He said to tell you goodbye and that he thought you were beautiful."

"He did? Oh!" she moaned. "This is so crazy. Is this Tim?"

I couldn't blame her for asking. He looked half-dead, bleeding over Nate's bed, hardly recognizable at all.

Mrs. Mackenzie was at the bedroom door.

"Nate?" she said with bewilderment spread across her face. "What's going on?"

The last time she saw us, Nate, Lucinda and I were with Willie, not Tim.

"Um, he's sick," Nate said. "I've called for an ambulance."

Mrs. Mackenzie walked over to the bed. "Oh my goodness, what happened to him?" She stared at his wound and then his face. "That's not the same boy you came in here with?" She turned to Nate. "Nate?"

"I'll explain later, Mom."

We heard knocking on the front door, and Mrs. Mackenzie left to answer it. I ran after her to direct the paramedics to Nate's room.

"What happened here?" one of them said. They immediately ran an IV, pushing a big needle into a vein in Tim's arm.

"We don't know," Nate answered. I nodded my head. Playing dumb was the best course of action under the circumstances.

"This is a gunshot wound? What kind of gun?"

No way was I going to say a nineteenth century musket.

Mrs. Mackenzie had squeezed back into the room. "I don't understand. What's going on?"

There was no time to try to answer her.

One of the paramedics said, "When did this happen? The infection looks severe."

Nate and I shared a look but kept our lips sealed.

"They're not talking, Ed," the second paramedic said. "Let's get this kid to the hospital."

"I'm his sister. I want to come along."

They agreed and Nate said he'd meet me at the hospital. I was happy to miss the interrogation he was about to face from his mother. I caught a glimpse of Lucinda before I left. She sat with her hands clasped on her lap, her head down, her long hair covering her face. Her shoulders shuddered with her sobs, and I was sorry I couldn't be there for her.

I'd never ridden in the back of an ambulance before. One of the paramedics climbed in the back, taking a seat opposite me in front of a row of medical machinery that flashed and blinked. He took Tim's pulse and listened to his heart, all the while talking to whoever it was that waited for us at the hospital.

The sirens screamed, and I hung on as the ambulance made quick turns.

"Casey," Tim moaned.

"I'm here." I squeezed his hand.

"I don't want to die."

"You're not going to die. We're back now and headed for Mount Auburn."

"They're not going to hack off my leg?"

"No." I smiled. "You'll live to walk again."

"Thank you." Tears ran down my brother's face and my throat swelled up. His lips tightened around his teeth as he worked to get the words out. "Thanks for coming after me. For not giving up."

"I'll never give up on you, Tim. I love you."

"I love you, too, sis."

34

CASEY

Three Days Later

TIM HAD A NASTY MAZE of stitches on his leg that would leave a scar to remind us all of the time we'd almost lost him. But, thankfully, the infection had subsided. My parents hadn't left his side since the operation, and I'd convinced them to go home for a couple of hours to get some rest. It was nice to finally be alone with Tim.

Tim picked at the hospital food on the tray in front of him.

"I didn't survive the Civil War to die of starvation in a modern hospital," he said. "You have to sneak me something better. A steak sandwich and a bag of chocolate-chip cookies."

I laughed. "Consider it done. And don't mention the war. They might lock you up."

We'd already cast a lot of suspicion because we were

unable to come up with a believable story. How did you properly explain where Tim had been for weeks, our lack of hygiene, and his unlikely wound?

There was a TV monitor hanging from the ceiling and the news report was on.

"Do you want me to turn it off?" I asked.

Tim nodded. Just before I pushed the button on the remote, a story broke about a gang bust in New York. Stories like this were a dime a dozen, and normally I wouldn't have given it a second glance, if not for the image of one of the gang members with a particular tattoo.

Apparently the story gave Tim an idea.

"I was sucked into a street gang. That's where I was when I was gone. There was a fight and I was caught in the cross-fire."

I raised an eyebrow. "That's your story?"

"It happened once–at the bank–it could happen again."

I nibbled on my cheek. It could work. It was a plausible story, and I had a feeling there was a basis of truth there.

Besides, we couldn't hold the police or my parents off much longer. They wanted answers.

"I'll let the others know."

The others being Lucinda and Nate.

I hadn't seen Nate since the night we arrived at the hospital. Once Tim had gotten out of surgery and we were told he'd be all right, all Nate and I wanted to do was go to our own beds and sleep. He called me the next day, but I didn't answer. He texted me throughout the day, but I ignored those, too. Gradually the calls and texts dwindled down to one or two, and none as of today.

It wasn't because I'd stopped loving him. If anything I loved him more, but I couldn't bear the thought that he'd stayed with me out of a sense of loyalty, because he knew about my life and somehow that made him responsible for me.

I'd miss him, but he deserved to live the life he wanted to live, not one he felt he had to live. I closed my eyes and pushed back the pain.

"Are you okay?" Tim said.

I forced a smile. "Yeah, I'm fine."

But there was still one question I needed answered. The catalyst to this whole nightmare.

I turned to Tim. "Who gave you the drugs?"

"Does it matter?"

"Yes, it does."

He nodded and I leaned in to hear his answer just as Mom and Dad walked in the hospital room door, each with a coffee cup in their hands.

AFTER A WHILE THE nurse shooed us all out so Tim could rest. Mom and Dad dropped me off at home before going off to their respective jobs. They felt rested and rest assured enough to put in a few hours of work, and I was glad to see them go back to doing something that resembled normal. Now that Tim was going to be fine, the heavy mood that had shrouded our house had lifted and life could find its regular rhythm once again.

Chase Miller was outside, ear buds in his ears, lounging in his favorite patio chair, wearing his signature jeans and tight T-shirt. I sauntered over the property line, my flip-flops making smacking noises and my heart racing just a little bit.

He looked at me from under his shades. "Howdy, neighbor."

"Hey," I said, offering a smile.

"How's your brother today?" His concern was touching.

"Better. He's getting stronger every day."

"I'm glad to hear it." He cocked his head and I couldn't help mimicking him. I pushed a loose curl behind my ear.

"So, are we on for dinner, yet?" he asked confidently.

I laughed. "I can't date you."

"Why? Don't tell me you still have that boyfriend?"

My heart sunk, but I didn't answer him. Instead I said, "I think you're going to be busy with other things."

He flashed me a Hollywood smile. "I only want to be busy with you."

Such a charmer. I didn't have time to respond because at that moment a police cruiser pulled into Chase's driveway. I recognized the officer who got out.

"Officer Porter," I called out. It was so good to see her back at work.

Chase ran a hand through his short cropped hair and breathed out in relief. "Oh, she's a friend of yours?"

I nodded. "Yeah." You could say that.

Clarice walked steadily toward us, thumbs hooked in the belt of her uniform. She smiled at me, her brown eyes growing soft. She reminded me of someone, but I couldn't place who just now.

"How's Tim?" she asked.

"He's good. Getting stronger."

"He's had quite the summer, hasn't he?"

"Yeah, he sure has."

Chase watched our exchange with interest.

"Oh, Officer Porter, I'd like you to meet my neighbor, Chase Miller."

Chase stood and offered his hand.

"That won't be necessary," she said. "Unless you'd like to offer them both." She dangled a set of handcuffs in front of Chase's bewildered face.

"Mr. Miller, I'd like you to come with me. You're under arrest for distributing drugs to minors."

"What? That's crazy?" Chase's eyes darted at me. "Did you call her?"

I had, in fact. Before I'd left the hospital.

"Tim and Alex confirmed that you approached them shortly after you moved in," I said.

I stared hard at the tattoo on his bicep, the raven, a symbol of a youth gang from New York. The same tattoo I'd spotted on the news story earlier. "You were recruiting members for your gang, and offered drugs as part of the buy-in."

Chase's jaw clenched and his lips formed a tight line. I imagined that he already knew all about not talking without a lawyer present. He went with Officer Porter without a fight, but instead of feeling victorious and smug as I watched his blond head through the window of the cruiser, I felt sad and empty.

I went inside and stood in the middle of the kitchen taking in all the quiet and order, and I felt unsure as to what I should do next. School started tomorrow, so I really needed to get ready for that. My cell rang as I headed up the stairs to my room. I checked the caller ID. Lucinda.

I picked it up.

"Hi, Luce."

"Hey. Just checking in, wondering how things are going."

I knew she was worried about me. I worried about her, too. Losing Willie suddenly like that wasn't easy.

"They're going okay," I answered. "How about you?"

"Fine, I guess."

I filled her in on the drama with Chase.

"No way. And he seemed so nice."

"Well..."

"Except for that part where he unabashedly moved in on you while you were with Nate."

I laughed a little. "Except for that part."

"You still haven't talked to him, have you?"

I reached my room and sat on the edge of my bed. "No."

"Casey."

"I know. I will soon. He's going back to class in Boston this week. I'll call tonight."

"Are you sure you want to do this?"

No. I wasn't sure. "I think it's already been done. He's stopped calling."

"Well, duh. If someone doesn't answer your calls, you have to take the hint."

I fell flat onto my back and closed my eyes. "It's for the best."

"If you think so. It's just that you two seemed so right for each other, you know?"

Thankfully the doorbell rang and I could end this agonizing call. "Sorry, someone's at the door. I have to go."

A strange man with a bouquet of flowers stood on the front patio step. He studied his notebook. "Casey Donovan?"

"Yes?"

"These are for you."

I took the flowers–a mix of red roses, daisies and blossoms I couldn't name. I opened up the little card, but all it said was "*I.*"

"I" what?

I carried the flowers to the kitchen and pulled a vase

from the corner cupboard. I no sooner had the bouquet in water when the doorbell rang again.

Another delivery, this time from a different flower company. This bouquet was bigger and brighter than the first. I ripped open the card.

"*Was*"

My heart started to flutter. I took these flowers to the kitchen, but I didn't even have time to find a vase before the doorbell rang again.

Another new guy and a new flower company. This bouquet was completely white. Roses, lilies, baby's breath. My hand trembled as I opened the card.

"*Wrong.*"

My eyes stung with tears. I searched the yard and up and down the street, but there was no one. I made my way back to the kitchen. Found two more vases, filled them with water and arranged the flowers.

Maybe I should call him.

The doorbell rang again.

Again?

No flower delivery guy this time, but there were flowers. The whole front patio was filled with flowers of every color and kind, like I'd opened my own floral shop.

Then Nate stepped out from around the corner. His hands were tucked in the pockets of his jeans, and his beautiful eyes looked up at me through gorgeous dark lashes. He mouthed the words, "Forgive me?"

I nodded and ran to him, wrapping my arms around his neck, breathing in the scent of him.

He cupped my cheeks in his hands and whispered. "I'm sorry I wasn't first. I always want to be your first."

His lips brushed mine, and I gasped, pulling him closer. I couldn't believe I almost let him go.

"Casey," Nate said between kisses. "Can you promise me something?"

"Anything."

"Don't pull away again. No matter how badly I screw up."

"I thought you wanted to go."

"I didn't and I don't. That will never change."

An explosion of happiness bubbled in my belly. "Okay. I promise."

We sat on the step and I snuggled close to him, breathing deeply of the floral scent that surrounded me.

"They're beautiful," I whispered.

He kissed my forehead and held me tight.

"By the way," he said. "Was it my imagination or did I see Chase Miller going for a ride in the back seat of Officer Porter's cruiser?"

I arched an eyebrow. "You've been staking out my neighborhood?"

His eyes twinkled. "Well, you know, undercover stuff. Operation Blossom."

"I see." I told him about Chase, and what a bad neighbor he'd turned out to be.

Nate scowled. "I knew that guy was trouble."

He was right. Note to self. Listen to Nate more often.

A cool wind stirred, a reminder that the seasons were about to change. I shivered and pressed into him, hating that this day would have to end.

"School tomorrow," I said. "I don't want you to leave."

"I'll be home every night and on weekends," he said. He cupped my chin in his hand. "It'll be like I'm not even gone."

"What about college girls?" I asked. "Do I need to worry about them?"

"Do I need to worry about high school guys? Criminals or otherwise?"

He brushed my lips with his.

"Nope," I said with a big, sappy grin. "You don't have to worry."

Don't miss out on the companion book, LIKE CLOCKWORK.

LIKE CLOCKWORK is a companion book to Clockwise and can be read alone.

Adeline shows up again with Casey in Counter Clockwise

Adeline doesn't feel she belongs in her own time, but can bad boys from the past be trusted?

Adeline Savoy had hoped that the move west from Cambridge to Hollywood with her single dad would mean they'd finally bond like a real family, but all she got was a father too busy with his new female friends and his passion for acting to really see her.

Instead, she finds herself getting attached to Faye, the divorcee hairdresser she befriends when she travels back in time to 1955. Plus Faye has a hottie, James Dean-esque, bad-boy brother who has Adeline's heart all aflutter. But bad boys from the past can be dangerous.

Is it possible that Adeline really does belong in her own time and that maybe the right boy lives as close as next door?

WHAT READERS ARE SAYING:

"LIKE CLOCKWORK IS as fun as the other books in the Clockwise series....I love this series and highly recommend it."

"GOOD TIME TRAVEL, cause and effect, fun twists, and clean! Characters are relatable. I wholeheartedly recommend the whole series!"

. . .

"THIS AUTHOR IS DANGEROUS, *lethal! Her books are totally addicting. Once you purchase the first you will not be able to stop yourself from buying the next.*"

Shop at leestraussbooks.com

Read on for an excerpt.

If you enjoyed reading *ClockwiseR*, please help others enjoy it too.

Lend it: This ebook is lending-enabled, so please share with a friend.

Recommend it: Help others find the book by recommending it to friends, readers' groups, discussion boards and by suggesting it to your local library.

Review it: Please tell other readers why you liked this book by reviewing it at **leestraussbooks.com**.

FOR MORE INFORMATION about my books or how to follow me on social media, visit leestraussbooks.com

ABOUT THE AUTHOR

Lee Strauss is a USA TODAY bestselling author of The Ginger Gold Mysteries series, The Higgins & Hawke Mystery series, The Rosa Reed Mystery series (cozy historical mysteries), A Nursery Rhyme Mystery series (mystery suspense), The Light & Love series (sweet romance), The Clockwise Collection (YA time travel romance), and young adult historical fiction with over a million books read. She has titles published in German and French, and a growing audio library.

When Lee's not writing or reading she likes to cycle, hike, and stare at the ocean. She loves to drink caffè lattes and red wines in exotic places, and eat dark chocolate anywhere.

For more info on books by Lee Strauss and her social media links, visit leestraussbooks.com. To make sure you don't miss the next new release, be sure to sign up for her readers' list!

Discuss the books, ask questions, share your opinions. Fun giveaways! Join the Lee Strauss Readers' Group on Facebook for more info.

Did you know you can follow your favourite authors on Bookbub? If you subscribe to Bookbub — (and if you don't, why don't you? - They'll send you daily emails alerting you to sales and new releases on just the kind of books you like to read!) — follow me to make sure you don't miss the next Ginger Gold Mystery!

www.leestraussbooks.com
leestraussbooks@gmail.com

LIKE CLOCKWORK

ADELINE SAVOY

MY DAD STILL thought I was ten. That was how old I was when my mother died, and how old I was when my father crawled into his "cave," also known as his office on the 26th floor of the John Hancock tower. Six years later, like a bear coming out of hibernation, Dad decided his days of hiding behind a desk were over. I thought he was going through a mid-life crisis, which was why we now lived in Hollywood instead of Cambridge. And why when I spotted his reflection in a mirror at the cosmetic counter in the Shop & Save store, I almost dropped the *Scarlet Passion* lipstick tester I'd just smeared on my lips.

Even though I was sixteen, I wasn't allowed to wear make-up. True. With my left hand I used a tissue to wipe the evidence off my mouth, all the while watching my dad's familiar profile move in and out of range in the mirror.

He was laughing. I crouched down and turned, my vision just missing the counter top, and watched. His hair had grown out since the "decision." He used to always keep it so short, that I didn't even know it was wavy before, and the lines on his face never used to turn upward in a smile.

I had to see who was causing this cosmic reaction in my father. The clerk who sold cheap jewelry, a pretty-in-a-fake way brunette, tilted her head and giggled back.

My jaw dropped and something really strange started happening in my stomach. I felt a little sick because I couldn't believe what I was witnessing. My dad was *flirting*!

Who was this man dressed in khakis, flip-flops and an un-tucked pseudo Hawaiian shirt? My real dad only wore pinstriped suits with starchy white shirts and a blue tie. Always. Even to bed, I was certain.

"Miss? Are you all right?" The cosmetic clerk was armed with a spray nozzle cleaner in one hand and a paper towel in the other.

I mimed as best I could, "ssh", but apparently dad was the only one with acting skills in my family, since she wouldn't leave me alone.

"Miss? You don't look too good. Should I call for medical?"

The fake pretty lady stopped chatting when she heard her colleague talking so loudly. Obviously, that meant my dad's little flirtation episode was over. And of course, my blonde ponytail was a giveaway. "Adeline?" he said.

"Dad!" I jumped up, feigning surprise.

"What are you doing here?" he asked.

What are you doing here? I thought. "Um nothing, just looking. Thought I might buy some gum."

Dad glanced back at the fake and I did a quick switcheroo, replacing the tester and grabbing a sealed golden tube. It tucked nicely in my fist as I crossed my arms over my chest.

"Adeline, come here," Dad said. "I want you to meet someone."

My legs moved toward dad and the fake without my permission.

"Adeline, this is my friend from acting class, Spring. Spring, this is my daughter, Adeline."

Spring extended her hand. Unfortunately, the contraband lipstick was in my right hand. I wasn't a magician. Dad would notice if I tried to switch. I opted for the awkward offering of my left hand.

"It's so nice to meet you," Spring gushed.

"Same," I said, not meaning it at all. "Not that I don't want to stay and chat," I added quickly, before Dad could draw us into more forced intimacies, "but I've got to go."

"I'll walk with you," Dad said. But he wasn't looking at me; he was smiling at the fake.

"It's okay, Dad. I'll meet you at home." I strutted across the floor to the cashier. He glanced back at me as I stood in line at the register. I waved the pack of gum in the air. I paid for it and the lipstick while Dad and the fake went back to making googly eyes.

I snapped the gum in my mouth while caressing the lipstick tube in my hand. It was encased in a plastic protective seal, a perforated strip running the length of it like a zipper. My thumb picked at the rim. All I had to do was rip it open and it would no longer be returnable.

But I really should return it. I'd promised myself I'd give up the greasy lip habit when we moved. It was a chance to start over, do everything new, and be a proper daughter with a proper father.

Harrumph. Like that was turning out. Dad wasn't exactly holding up his end of the bargain.

My breaths came out short and rapid, like a panting dog. I didn't realize how fast I'd been walking. I'd hardly taken in the tall palm trees that lined the road or the sweet smell of tropical flowers I didn't know the names of.

No signs of autumn in sight. In Cambridge the leaves would be showing signs of turning color, bright reds and yellows. A little twist in my stomach. I was homesick.

And angry.

He was supposed to change, but not like that. He was supposed to notice me, spend time with me, not some flake called Spring. What kind of name was that anyway? It sounded like a made up actress name. Her last name was probably Storm or Wind. My thumb picked the plastic a bit more.

"Hi, there."

I turned my head. Some guy riding a pink bike with a sparkly white banana seat and matching tassels that hung off tall, wide handlebars slowed down to keep pace with me.

"Hi," he said again. This time there was no mistaking he was talking to me.

"Hi?" I said, not slowing down at all to do so. I may be entering my junior year, but I still didn't talk to strangers. Janice, my babysitter/pseudo mom in Cambridge, had drilled that lesson into me good.

"My name's Marco. I live next door to you."

Okay. I slowed a little. "Why are you riding a girl's bike?" Did he steal it? Why didn't he care about how stupid it made him look?

"It's my sister's. I sold mine to buy something else, but riding this is better than walking."

"I'm walking and you're not making any better time than me." I was annoyed. Why didn't he just keep going? I preferred to sulk alone.

"You're new, so I thought with school starting tomorrow, you'd like someone to ride the bus with."

Good point. Who knew what kinds of Hollywood weirdos would be on the bus? I looked Marco up and down. He was average height, shaggy hair, and wore a graphic T-shirt and surfer shorts with fat, loosely tied skate shoes on his feet. No socks. He had nice, tanned skin and warm brown eyes that squinted to almost close when he smiled. He wasn't hard to look at.

And he looked trustworthy enough, I guessed. Plus, he was right. I didn't really want to go to Hollywood High alone.

I stopped and turned to him. "I'm Adeline Savoy." I wiped the sweat on my right hand off on my skirt—sky blue, slightly flared and to my knees—and offered it wanting to start my new friendship off on the right foot.

"Cool," Marco said as we shook. "You like to make things official. I like that."

The sun must've glinted off the gold tube in my other hand because Marco nodded toward it. "What'ya got there?"

"Oh, it's just lipstick. I bought it, but now I'm not sure. I might take it back."

"I don't know why girls wear that vile stuff," he said. I was surprised by the strength of his statement.

"It makes us feel good. Pretty. What's wrong with that?"

"For one thing, you're already pretty without it."

He thought I was pretty?

"Besides," he continued, "it's made out of horse urine."

"It is not! That's so gross."

"It is. That's why it has that sticky consistency. Have you ever seen dried urine around a toilet?"

"You're disgusting! How would you know about lipstick, anyway?"

"I have three sisters, though one is only six years old and hasn't discovered the evils of make-up and this culture's drive to sexualize young girls. It's too late for my older sisters, but you can still be saved."

Who was this guy? And how did he get off talking to me like that? He didn't even know me.

I felt my lips settle into a tight line and my pace picked up.

"Hey, I'm sorry. I didn't mean to offend you."

How long was he going to walk with me? "Where did you say you lived?"

"Right next door to you."

"Right next door?" This annoying person, who happened to be my only friend, lived right next door?

"Yeah, the two-storey. My bedroom window faces yours."

"You see in my window!"

"No. I don't..." His face flushed red.

"You do, you *do* look in. You peeping Tom!"

"Adeline, I didn't see anything. I just heard your music."

"Huh?" I stopped and spun to face him.

A grin tugged at the corners of his mouth. "And your singing."

"What?" I was mortified. He probably heard me singing along to *Feist*, or even worse, he saw me doing my Michael Jackson impersonation. I bet he saw me doing the *Thriller* dance the other night. Ugh!

"Everyone can hear you. You have your window open."

"You know what? Don't talk to me."

Marco seemed truly taken aback, and yet he didn't get the hint. Not even one as direct as that. He was not only a peeper, but he was dense, too.

"I live in a house full of women. Three sisters and a mother. I get what's going on here. It's PMS, isn't it?"

Was he *kidding* me? As if I would talk about something like that with him! I stopped and stared hard into his eyes. I produced my new tube of lipstick and slowly peeled the perforated strip, letting the plastic wrapper drop to the ground. I dramatically popped off the lid and twisted the base until the bright red dried horse urine was in full view.

Then I put it on my lips, slowly, purposefully, first the top and then the bottom, smacking them in Marco's direction when I was done.

Take that, Mr. I Know Women.

Marco bent down, picked up the plastic wrapper and pushed it in his pocket. He straddled the bike and pushed off, turning back long enough to say, "I'll pick you up at 8:10 tomorrow morning for school."

Argh.

Shop at leestraussbooks.com

MORE FROM LEE STRAUSS

Shop at leestraussbooks.com

GINGER GOLD MYSTERY SERIES (cozy 1920s historical)

Cozy. Charming. Filled with Bright Young Things. This Jazz Age murder mystery will entertain and delight you with its 1920s flair and pizzazz!

Murder on the SS Rosa

Murder at Hartigan House

Murder at Bray Manor

Murder at Feathers & Flair

Murder at the Mortuary

Murder at Kensington Gardens

Murder at St. George's Church

The Wedding of Ginger & Basil

Murder Aboard the Flying Scotsman

Murder at the Boat Club

Murder on Eaton Square

Murder by Plum Pudding

Murder on Fleet Street

Murder at Brighton Beach

Murder in Hyde Park

Murder at the Royal Albert Hall

Murder in Belgravia

Murder on Mallowan Court

Murder at the Savoy

Murder at the Circus

Murder in France

Murder at Yuletide

Murder at Madame Tussauds

LADY GOLD INVESTIGATES (Ginger Gold companion short stories)

Volume 1

Volume 2

Volume 3

Volume 4

Volume 5

HIGGINS & HAWKE MYSTERY SERIES (cozy 1930s historical)

The 1930s meets Rizzoli & Isles in this friendship depression era cozy mystery series.

Death at the Tavern

Death on the Tower

Death on Hanover

Death by Dancing

THE ROSA REED MYSTERIES

(1950s cozy historical)

Murder at High Tide

Murder on the Boardwalk

Murder at the Bomb Shelter

Murder on Location

Murder and Rock 'n Roll

Murder at the Races

Murder at the Dude Ranch

Murder in London

Murder at the Fiesta

Murder at the Weddings

A NURSERY RHYME MYSTERY SERIES(mystery/sci fi)

Marlow finds himself teamed up with intelligent and savvy Sage Farrell, a girl so far out of his league he feels blinded in her presence - literally - damned glasses! Together they work to find the identity of @gingerbreadman. Can they stop the killer before he strikes again?

Gingerbread Man

Life Is but a Dream

Hickory Dickory Dock

Twinkle Little Star

LIGHT & LOVE (sweet romance)

Set in the dazzling charm of Europe, follow Katja, Gabriella, Eva, Anna and Belle as they find strength, hope and love.

Love Song

Your Love is Sweet

In Light of Us

Lying in Starlight

PLAYING WITH MATCHES (WW2 history/romance)

A sobering but hopeful journey about how one young German boy copes with the war and propaganda. Based on true events.

A Piece of Blue String (companion short story)

THE CLOCKWISE COLLECTION (YA time travel romance)

Casey Donovan has issues: hair, height and uncontrollable trips to the 19th century! And now this ~ she's accidentally taken Nate Mackenzie, the cutest boy in the school, back in time. Awkward.

Clockwise

Clockwiser

Like Clockwork

Counter Clockwise

Clockwork Crazy

Clocked (companion novella)

Standalones

Seaweed

Love, Tink

ACKNOWLEDGMENTS

I have to thank my family first, for believing in me and cheering me on, especially my daughter Tasia and my husband Norm. Your unwavering support means so much to me. A huge shout out to my wattpad fans! If it weren't for your calls for a sequel, Clockwiser wouldn't exist and I'm so glad it does!

Thanks to my beta readers, Lori, Angelika, Sandra and Bethany for reassuring me that I was on the right track, and to my editor Leigh Moore for making it sing. A special thanks to Alice Lynn and Eryn LaPlant Rask for your comments and guidance on authenticity. My Friday morning Noble Girls —you rock! Thank YOU, reader for making time in your lives for Casey and Nate and for loving them (I hope) as much as I do. =) And always to God. I'm so glad I'm not alone in all of this.